MEET THE FORTUNES:

Fortune of the Month: Graham Fortune

Age: 32

Vital statistics: Broad heart as big as Texas.

Claim to fame: Graham multimillion-dollar busin the Galloping G. His fath say ne has "untapped potential." Graham believes he is already living the dream.

Romantic prospects: Impossible. He's crushing on his childhood buddy Sasha-Marie Smith. She has a seven-year-old daughter and is expecting a second one. Did we mention that she is technically still married? Her soon-to-be ex walked out on her and she's seven months pregnant. He's sure romance is the very last thing on her mind.

"I've never done what anyone has expected of me. I'm a cowboy in a family of computer geeks. I'd rather punch a cow than a time clock. And I'd rather live alone than settle.

So now I've finally found my Miss Right. But the timing is absolutely wrong. Sasha has a baby on the way. Maybe she's still stuck on her ex. And for sure she doesn't think of me as anything other than a friend. What kind of guy pursues a woman who's got so much weighing on her slender shoulders?

On the other hand, what self-respecting cowboy can ignore a beautiful damsel in distress?"

THE FORTUNES OF TEXAS:
ALL FORTUNE'S CHILDREN—
Money. Family. Cowboys.
Meet the Austin Fortunes!

Dear Reader,

I'm delighted to be a part of the 2016 Fortunes of Texas 20th Anniversary continuity. I've written quite a few Fortunes books, and as you probably know, the stories just keep getting better and better. *Wed by Fortune* is book six and will wrap up this series. (But don't worry—with several unattached Fortune Robinson siblings still looking for love, there just might be another series in the works!)

This book is the story of Graham Fortune Robinson, who is helping his late friend's father create a home for rescued horses and wayward teens. His love match is Sasha-Marie Gibault, a pregnant single mom who once had a secret crush on Graham when he was a rebellious teen himself. As is often the case, Graham thought of Sasha as a kid and didn't give her the time of day. But all that changes the moment Sasha shows up on the Galloping G after being away for years, all grown-up and gorgeous. She's still harboring those girlish feelings for Graham—only they're not girlish anymore.

If you like stories about ranchers, single pregnant moms and the revelation of family secrets, you're going to enjoy reading *Wed by Fortune* as much as I enjoyed writing it!

Wishing you romance!

Judy Duarte

PS: I love hearing from my readers. You can contact me on Facebook at Facebook.com/judyduartenovelist.

Wed by Fortune

Judy Duarte

HARLEQUIN®SPECIAL EDITION®

Special thanks and acknowledgment to Judy Duarte
for her contribution to the
Fortunes of Texas: All Fortune's Children continuity.

Recycling programs
for this product may
not exist in your area

978-0-373-65961-6

Wed by Fortune

Copyright © 2016 by Harlequin Books S.A.

HARLEQUIN®
www.Harlequin.com

Printed in U.S.A.

Since 2002, *USA TODAY* bestselling author **Judy Duarte** has written over forty books for Harlequin Special Edition, earned two RITA® Award nominations, won two MAGGIE® Awards and received a National Reader's Choice Award. When she's not cooped up in her writing cave, she enjoys traveling with her husband and spending quality time with her grandchildren. You can learn more about Judy and her books at her website, judyduarte.com, or at Facebook.com/judyduartenovelist.

Books by Judy Duarte

Harlequin Special Edition

Brighton Valley Cowboys

The Cowboy's Double Trouble
Having the Cowboy's Baby
The Boss, the Bride & the Baby

Return to Brighton Valley

The Soldier's Holiday Homecoming
The Bachelor's Brighton Valley Bride
The Daddy Secret

The Fortunes of Texas: Cowboy Country

A Royal Fortune

The Fortunes of Texas: Welcome to Horseback Hollow

A House Full of Fortunes!

The Fortunes of Texas: Southern Invasion

Marry Me, Mendoza

Byrds of a Feather

Tammy and the Doctor

Visit the Author Profile page
at Harlequin.com for more titles.

Chapter One

Graham Robinson had spent the morning working up a good sweat, thanks to a drunken teenager who'd gotten behind the wheel of a Cadillac Escalade after a rowdy, unsupervised party last night.

The kid had apparently lost control of the expensive, late-model SUV and plowed through a large section of the fence at the Galloping G Ranch, where Graham lived. Then he left the vehicle behind and ran off.

Both Graham and the sheriff who'd been here earlier knew it had been a teenager because on the passenger seat a frayed backpack, as well as a catcher's mitt, sat next to an invitation with directions to a ranch six miles down the road.

Sadly, the same thing could easily have happened to him, when he'd been seventeen. That's why he and

Roger Gibault, his friend and the owner of the ranch, were determined to turn the Galloping G into a place where troubled teenage boys could turn their lives around.

Back in the day, both Graham and Roger's late son had what Roger called rebellious streaks. Graham's dad, the patriarch of the famous Austin Robinsons—and an alleged member of the Fortune family—wasn't so open-minded.

But after Peter's tragic death, things had changed. Graham had changed. Now, instead of creating problems for others to clean up, Graham was digging out several damaged posts and replacing broken railings.

After he hammered one last nail into the rail he'd been fixing, he blew out a sigh and glanced at the well-trained Appaloosa gelding that was grazing nearby on an expanse of green grass. He'd driven out here earlier in the twelve-year-old Gator ATV, but the engine had been skipping. So after unloading his tools and supplies, he'd taken it back to the barn, where Roger could work on the engine. Then he'd ridden back on the gelding. Hopefully, Roger had the vehicle fixed by now. If not, they'd probably have to replace it with a newer model.

When the familiar John Deere engine sounded, Graham looked over his shoulder. Sure enough, Roger had worked his mechanical magic and was approaching at a fairly good clip.

Moments later, the aging rancher pulled to a stop, the engine idling smoothly.

Glad to have a break, Graham winked at his elderly

friend. "Did you come out here to check up on me and make sure I wasn't loafing?"

"I knew better than that. I'd be more apt to make sure you hadn't worked yourself to death." Roger lifted his battered black Stetson, then raked a hand through his thinning gray hair.

The fact that he hadn't returned Graham's smile was cause for concern. "What's up?"

Roger paused for a beat, then said, "Sasha-Marie just called. She's on her way here."

Graham nearly dropped the hammer he was holding. Roger and his niece had once been close, but they'd drifted apart after her marriage. "Is she still living in California?"

"I don't think so. But I'm not sure."

When Sasha-Marie had been in kindergarten, she lost her parents in a small plane crash. Her maternal grandparents, who lived in Austin, were granted custody, but she spent many of her school vacations with Roger, her paternal uncle.

Since Roger and his late wife had only one child, a son who'd been born to them late in life, Sasha-Marie became the daughter they'd never had and the apple of her doting uncle's eye.

Roger had been proud when she went off to college, but he hadn't approved of the man she'd met there and started dating. After she married the guy and moved out of state, Roger rarely mentioned her.

Graham hadn't met her husband. He'd been invited to the wedding, although he hadn't attended. He'd come down with a nasty stomach flu and had stayed on the ranch.

According to Roger, it had been a "big wingding," and most likely the sort of elegant affair that Graham's family usually put on, the kind of function he still did his best to avoid whenever possible.

On the morning of the wedding, as Graham had gone to replenish a glass of water, he'd met Roger in the Galloping G kitchen. Roger had been dressed in a rented tuxedo, his hair slicked back, his lips pursed in a scowl. His job was to give away the bride, but he hadn't been happy about it.

"This ain't right," he'd said.

Graham thought he might be talking about the monkey suit he'd been asked to wear. "You mean all the wedding formalities?"

Roger shook his head and clucked his tongue. "I tried to talk her out of it, but she won't hear it. Just because she's gone off to college, she thinks she's bright. But she's been so blinded by all the glitz and glamour she can't see what a louse her future husband really is."

Having grown up in tech mogul Gerald Robinson's household, Graham had experienced plenty of glitz and glamour himself. He knew a lot of phony people who flashed their wealth, which was one reason he was content to be a cowboy and manage the Galloping G for Roger.

The other reason was that he wanted to look out for the old rancher and his best interests. That's why the news of Sasha's return today was a big deal.

"Is Sasha's husband coming with her?" Graham asked.

"Nope." Roger placed his hat back on his head, adjusting it properly and shading his eyes from the afternoon sun.

Graham wondered if the older man would offer up another comment, but he kept his thoughts to himself. That really wasn't surprising. He'd been pretty close-lipped about Sasha since the wedding, which must have been eight or more years ago. Graham had tried to get him to talk about his anger and disappointment, thinking that might help. But he respected the man's silence. He also sympathized with him.

After Sasha gave birth to a baby—a girl, if Graham remembered correctly—Roger had gone to visit her in California. He'd not only wanted to see his great-niece, but he'd also hoped to mend fences. Two days later he'd returned to the ranch, just as quiet as he'd been before. Graham's only clue to what had transpired was the response to his single question about how things went.

"Not well," Roger had said. And that had pretty much been the end of it.

Graham stole a glance at the man who'd become more of a father to him than his own dad. But then again, they'd weathered Peter's death together, leaning on each other so they could get through the gut-wrenching, heartbreaking grief.

Bonds like that were strong. And they lasted a lifetime.

Roger stared out in the distance at the two-lane highway that led to the big ranch house in which he now lived alone. Was he looking for Sasha's car?

Or was he just pondering the blowup that he'd had with her husband? Graham wasn't privy to all that had happened on Sasha's wedding day, but he did know that Gabe had, in so many words, told Roger to butt out of Sasha's life.

So the rift had always weighed heavily on his mind—and it probably still did.

"It's a good sign that she felt like she could call and talk to you," Graham said.

"I agree." Roger heaved a heavy sigh. "She didn't tell me what brought about the sudden change of heart, but that doesn't matter."

"Either way, for your sake, I'm glad she's coming without her husband."

Roger snorted. "I always figured Gabe for a fast-talking womanizer who'd end up breaking her heart down the road. But that didn't mean I didn't want to be proven wrong."

"You won't hold any of that against Sasha, will you?"

"Hell no. I'd never do that. But I'll tell you, Graham, it hurt like a son of a gun when she left Texas. And while I'm glad she reached out to me just now, I'm leery about pushing myself on her too quickly."

Whatever had gone down between Roger and the groom at the church had nearly destroyed the relationship Roger once had with his niece.

"How long is she going to be here?" Graham asked. He assumed it'd be for a few days to a week.

"I don't have the foggiest idea, but I told her she could stay as long as she wanted."

Sasha had been a cute kid. She'd tagged along after Graham and Peter when they were teenagers, wanting to be included—and being a pest more times than not. She was probably close to thirty now, but Graham would always remember her as a skinny young girl with braces and a scatter of freckles across her nose.

Roger glanced out to the road again, squinting as he scanned the empty stretch of blacktop.

"Do you know what kind of car she drives?" Graham asked.

"Nope." The older man turned, sporting a wry grin. "I guess it's pretty obvious that I'm watching for her to arrive."

"Just a bit."

When a car engine sounded in the distance and grew louder, both men turned and spotted a white Honda Civic heading down the road. A blonde woman was driving, although the car was too far away to get a glimpse of her face.

"That might be Sasha-Marie now," Roger said.

It was hard to know for sure, although Roger was clearly eager to have her back on the Galloping G, no matter how short her stay.

"I'll finish up here," Graham said. "Why don't you go back to the house so you can greet her?"

"Nope. I want you to come with me. You can get those tools later. Mount up."

Graham scanned the fence he'd been working on, realizing it wasn't going anywhere. And apparently, neither was that Escalade if he enclosed it in the pasture before the owner came to claim it.

"All right," he said, "but why do you want me to be there?"

Roger scowled and rolled his eyes. "Because I never have been able to keep my opinions to myself. And if I slip up and say 'I told you so' or something negative about that jerk she's married to, I'll probably make things worse than they already are. So if you think I'm about to blurt out something like that, I want you to give me a wallop upside the head."

Roger had a point. He was a good man, hardworking and honest to a fault. But he'd never been one to hold back an opinion, no matter how rough it was around the edges. So Graham left his tools near the post he'd just cemented back into place, grabbed the Appaloosa's reins and swung into the saddle. "Okay, then. Let's go."

Neither of them knew for sure if the blonde driver had been Sasha, but on the outside chance that it was, they'd both be welcoming her home.

Sasha Gibault Smith parked near Uncle Roger's big white barn, but she didn't get out of the car right away. Instead, even though she needed to stretch her legs, she remained seated, gripping the steering wheel and studying the ranch she used to love to visit.

She'd started out from Los Angeles yesterday morning and had spent the night in El Paso, but it had still been a difficult trip, one she'd made with her tail tucked between her legs.

She adored Uncle Roger, but whenever she'd gone

against his advice, he'd had a habit of saying, "I told you so" or "Dang it, girl. Why don't you ever listen to me?" And this time, he'd been especially right in his assessment of Gabe Smith.

Needless to say, she wasn't looking forward to adding any additional guilt to what she already carried, especially now. That was one reason she'd been reluctant to call her uncle until she was only thirty minutes away.

She hadn't gone into detail about why she was coming back to Texas. Nor had she apologized for anything she or her now-estranged husband had done to hurt him. She'd merely asked if she could stay with him on the Galloping G for a while.

Before answering her question, he'd had one of his own. "Is Gabe coming with you?"

She'd said no, that it was just her and Maddie, and left it at that. She hadn't been ready to tell him any more over the phone.

"Stay as long as you want," Uncle Roger had said. "The city isn't a good place to raise a child." At that point, he'd paused, maybe rethinking his response. "I mean, city life is okay. Lots of cultural stuff and shopping, I suppose. But the fresh air and sunshine will be good for Maddie."

Bless his heart, Roger was the gruffest yet kindest man she'd ever known. And she was looking forward to mending their relationship, something she should have done a long time ago. But Gabe had made it so difficult. He'd made *everything* difficult.

She glanced into the rearview mirror to the backseat, where Maddie dozed. Her seven-year-old daughter was the only good thing that had come of her relationship with Gabe, so how could she regret marrying him?

But still, why hadn't she listened to Uncle Roger when he warned her about him?

Because she'd been dazzled by Gabe's charm and enamored with the very idea of love, that's why. She'd lost her parents when she was young, and all she'd ever wanted was to create a family of her own. But that dream had certainly backfired on her.

She'd been a fool not to see the truth. Gabe hadn't been capable of loving anyone but himself. And the fact that she'd signed the prenuptial agreement he'd said would appease his wealthy father only made it worse. What would Roger have said to *that*?

She could only imagine. She placed a hand on her growing baby bump, which had made it more difficult to reach the gas pedal, as well as the steering wheel, since she was merely five foot two, anyway.

The second pregnancy not only had led to her and Gabe's split, but had also complicated things. Gabe, who hadn't really wanted to have kids, would have to provide financially for both of them. His family came from money, so that hadn't bothered him nearly as much as the idea of coming home day after day to Sasha and the kids.

In fact, once Maddie was born, he began spending more and more time at the office. Sasha tried not to resent his time away from home since he'd said he was doing it for them, that he was only trying to be a good provider for his family. And maybe that was true. But she'd soon realized that Gabe was a quitter. Whenever something didn't go the way he liked it, he'd move on to another job.

The poor baby she was carrying, another little girl, hadn't asked to be brought into the world. But Gabe had barely gotten used to having Maddie. So when he found out Sasha was expecting again, he packed his bags and moved out.

It's not like she had intended to get pregnant this time. In fact, she still marveled at how it had even happened, since she and Gabe were so rarely together.

But none of that mattered. Her only priority now was her children. Come hell or high water, Sasha would do everything in her power to provide her daughters with love and security. And what better place to do that than at the Galloping G?

She just hoped Uncle Roger would agree. Her heart told her he would, but she'd never know until she broached the subject.

Again, she glanced in the rearview mirror. She didn't want to wake Maddie from her nap quite yet. The little girl hadn't felt comfortable in that motel room last night and had taken a long time to fall asleep. So to provide Maddie a few extra minutes to snooze in comfort, Sasha lowered the power windows to allow the afternoon breeze to blow through the car. Then she pulled the key from the ignition and placed it in her purse.

Before she could open the driver's door, a John Deere Gator drove into the yard, followed by a cowboy on horseback.

The man driving the Gator was Uncle Roger. And the cowboy…?

A Stetson shielded his face, but not his broad shoulders and rugged build. When he tilted the brim, she recognized Graham Robinson, and her breath caught.

His saddle creaked when he placed his hands on the pommel and leaned forward, checking her out without the hint of a smile. But she wasn't smiling, either. Talking to Uncle Roger would be hard enough without an audience.

What was Graham doing here? Hadn't he kicked his cowboy stage by now? Shouldn't he be working at Robinson Tech, raking in the dough and living the fast-paced urban life he'd been born into?

Not that he hadn't practically lived on the Galloping G during the summers when she used to come and visit. Graham and her cousin Peter had been best friends— and almost inseparable. Then, after Peter died, Graham had practically moved in.

She'd had a huge crush on the older teenage boy back then, but he'd only considered her a kid and a nuisance. In retrospect, she could understand why. He'd had his choice of high school girls. Why would he take a second look at her?

Besides, he and Peter were always talking about parties and all the places local teenagers hung out. Once she'd even heard them mention something about skinny-dipping with a couple of cheerleaders. So, no, Graham had never looked at her as anything other than a pesky little kid.

Uncle Roger approached first, which didn't surprise her. He was, after all, the one she'd come to see.

She tore her gaze from Graham, a wealthy man by all

rights who appeared to be more comfortable on horseback than in a snazzy BMW, something he could well afford to buy. At least, he'd never been without a wad of cash in the past. His dad owned a big tech company and had been loaded. He probably still was.

When Roger reached her car, Sasha was reluctant to get out. She hadn't told him about her pregnancy, although he was about to find out.

He took off his hat, revealing more silver in his hair than the last time she'd seen him. His face had weathered, too.

Her heart cramped at the thought that she and Gabe might have contributed to the signs of age.

"How was the drive?" he asked.

She lifted her hand to her eyes, blocking the glare from the afternoon sun. "It was long. But not too bad."

Uncle Roger took a peek into the backseat. "Looks like Maddie dozed off. You gonna wake her up?"

"I hadn't wanted to. She didn't sleep well last night. We stayed in a roadside motel, which had a truck stop next door, so it was pretty loud outside. But she's been eager to get here. And to meet you. It's all she could talk about."

As Uncle Roger studied her sweet, dozing daughter, Sasha stole another glance at Graham. He was dismounting now.

The years had been good to him, and as he swung a muscular leg over the saddle, all those girlish feelings returned tenfold. For one crazy, thoughtless moment, that silly crush she'd once harbored came rushing back full force and nearly stole her breath away.

She'd never met a man who could hold a candle to Graham in looks. In fact, if she weren't seven months pregnant and still—at least, *legally*—married, she'd be a goner.

Well, that wasn't true. She was older and wiser these days. And she'd learned the hard way that no man was perfect. Besides, she'd be swearing off romance and concentrating on her children for the next couple of years.

"You gonna sit in that car all day?" her uncle asked.

No, she wasn't about to do that. And while she wasn't eager to reveal her condition to either Roger or to Graham, she opened the door, grabbed her purse and slid out of her trusty Honda Civic.

The moment she did, Uncle Roger let out a slow whistle. But it wasn't Roger's reaction that concerned her now. For some dumb reason, she looked straight at Graham and waited for his response.

The first thing Graham noticed when Sasha got out of the car and stepped into the afternoon sunlight was that she was no longer the cute little tomboy he remembered. She was a stunning blonde and absolutely beautiful.

But damn. She was also *pregnant*. And while he was no expert, from the looks of it, she was about ready to deliver.

Were women in her condition supposed to travel, especially on long road trips?

Roger stepped away from Sasha's car, then strode toward Graham and reached out his hand. "Gimme those reins. I'll take care of your horse."

What the hell? And leave Graham to make small talk?

He would have objected and insisted on putting the horse away himself, but Roger was probably afraid to stick around any longer for fear he'd say something to screw things up before he got a chance to take Sasha's luggage inside. Speaking of which...

"Let me get your bags," Graham said.

"They're back here." Sasha, with the strap of her purse over her shoulder and her hand perched on her belly, rounded the car and opened her trunk.

She hadn't brought much, just two suitcases, so maybe she didn't plan to stay long.

"Is this it?" he asked.

"I...uh..." She gave a shrug. "I shipped everything else."

Everything? What all had she thought she'd need? Was she going to move in?

He lifted both bags from the car, and she shut the trunk. As he carried the suitcases to the front porch, he stole a peek at the lovely blonde.

Somewhere along the way, she'd shed the braces. And in spite of her obvious pregnancy, she'd blossomed into a shapely woman, one he found incredibly attractive. His heart rate had escalated to the point he felt what could almost be classified a sexual thrill just looking at her.

What did that say about *him*? What kind of man found a pregnant married woman so appealing?

He wasn't going to stew about it. Instead he shook off the question, as well as any answer he might be able to come up with. He was just surprised to see her and how much she'd changed, that's all.

"Is your daughter going to be okay in the car?" he asked.

"I'm only going to leave her in there for a minute. I thought I'd put my bags into the room where I used to sleep. But maybe I'd better leave them in the living room until Uncle Roger tells me where he'd like us to stay. I didn't mean to be presumptive."

"I'm sure it's fine to put everything in your old bedroom," Graham said, leading the way.

As far as he knew, Roger hadn't changed a thing since Sasha was last here, the summer of her junior year. He'd wanted things to stay the way she'd left them. But after her high school graduation, she'd stayed in Austin to prepare for college.

So she could easily see that the room with lavender walls, dotted with posters, still bore evidence of the teenager she'd once been.

Graham placed the bags on the bed, which boasted a white goose-down comforter.

Sasha set her purse on the antique oak dresser, then thanked him for his help.

"No problem."

They merely stood there, caught up in some kind of weird time warp. Then she nodded toward the doorway. "I'd better go wake up Maddie."

Graham followed her outside, watching her walk, the hem of her yellow sundress swishing against her shapely calves. From behind, he'd never have known she was expecting a baby.

When they reached the front porch, she paused near the railing, took a deep breath of country air and scanned the yard. "I've really missed this place."

Roger would be glad to know that. It would make it easier for them to put the past behind them.

"It's been a long time," Graham said, finally addressing the elephant in the room. "How've you been?"

"All right." She turned to face him and bit down on her bottom lip, as though things might not be "all right." But if that was the case, she didn't mention it. "How about you? I see you're still hanging out on the Galloping G."

"I live here now. In the foreman's quarters. I guess you could say I'm your uncle's right-hand man."

She pondered that bit of news for a moment. "I guess some things haven't changed."

Actually, she was wrong. A lot had changed, and there were more big changes coming down the pike.

"So, how's your family?" she asked.

"Same old, same old." It was a stock response to keep from going into any real detail. Sasha didn't know that he'd never been close to his father—and even less so now that he'd chosen not to work at Robinson Tech, like most of his other siblings.

When she nodded, he offered a more interesting response and something she might soon hear from the neighbors. "My brother Ben and my sisters Rachel and Zoe have gotten married recently. And my brother Wes is engaged."

"That's nice," she said, providing her own stock response. "How recently?"

"All within the last six months." Then, for some damn reason, he added, "We might also be taking on a new last name."

Her brow furrowed. "What do you mean?"

Since it was too late to backpedal now, he continued with the unsettling truth. "Apparently, my dad was once a long-lost black sheep in the Fortune clan. His name was Jerome, not Gerald."

Graham decided not to mention that Ben and some of his other siblings had taken on the Fortune name. But he wasn't about to do that, especially when his father refused to admit the connection.

"Wow," Sasha said. "And you never knew?"

"No, Dad kept that a secret from us, along with other things." Graham wasn't about to go into all that. Not now, anyway. Maybe not ever. He wasn't particularly proud of the fact that his old man, a guy most people considered a quirky tech mogul, had eight legitimate kids, as well as who-knew-how-many illegitimate ones.

"How do you feel about that?" she asked, easing close enough for him to catch the faint hint of her orange-blossom scent.

He blew out a sigh, hoping to eliminate the taunting smell, as well as his lingering concerns of being a shirttail relative to such a famous family. It didn't work in either case.

"It's been a lot for me to take in," he admitted. "So now my life on the Galloping G holds an even bigger appeal than it did before."

"I can imagine. News like that would be…stunning. How do your brothers and sisters feel about it?"

"Actually, some of them hope it's true. But the others aren't too keen on it." Graham, of course, was on the not-exactly-pleased side of it.

He paused for a beat, realizing Sasha didn't have siblings—or even a cousin any longer. So he didn't want to sound as though he resented having a big family. "I suppose you can never have too many relatives. It's a cold world out there, so the more people who have your back, the better."

Instead of smiling or commenting, Sasha just stood there as tears welled in her eyes.

Uh-oh. He hadn't meant to trigger her sadness. Was she missing Peter? Her parents?

She swiped below her eyes with the backs of her hands. "I'm sorry. Just the result of my pregnancy hormones at work."

That made sense. And it made him feel a lot better about setting off her tears. "How far along are you?"

"Seven months."

"Your husband must be thrilled."

Sasha glanced down at her sandals and didn't speak or look up for several beats.

He must have put his foot in his mouth again, although he had no idea why. Was she unhappy about the baby?

"I'm sorry if I was out of line," Graham said.

Sasha shook her head. When she looked up and caught his gaze, her eyes were glossy. "Gabe and I…

split up." Her hand again went to her belly, caressing the mound where her baby grew. "Actually, he left me."

Graham couldn't imagine what would cause a man to walk away from his family when his wife was pregnant. He'd never met Gabe Smith himself, but Roger had. And the old rancher's opinion of the guy was enough for Graham to believe the worst about him.

He'd never reveal that to Sasha, though. So he said, "That must be rough."

"We're doing okay. And on the upside, I'm now able to come visit Uncle Roger. Maddie is excited to see a real ranch—and horses."

Before Graham could respond, a little girl sidled up between them. She stuck out her hand to Graham and smiled, revealing a missing front tooth. "Howdy. Put 'er there, cowboy!"

He was captivated by her happy expression, by the long blond hair and bright blue eyes, so like her mama's.

What kind of man would leave such an adorable duo? Not that Graham had ever had any reason to admire Gabe Smith. But surely he'd come to his senses and chase after them.

For some strange reason, that thought caused his gut to clench, and he found it nearly impossible to speak. He did, however, reach out and take the child's little hand in his.

"You must be Maddie," he said.

"Yep." The girl stood tall, a big ol' grin stretching across her face. "And *you* must be Uncle Roger."

Chapter Two

Apparently, Maddie had awakened from her nap and gotten out of the car on her own. And while the little girl had no way of knowing who Graham or even Uncle Roger were, the idea that anyone could possibly confuse the two men brought a smile to Sasha's lips.

She placed her hand on the top of her daughter's head, her fingers trailing along the silky, pale strands. "This isn't Uncle Roger, Maddie. It's his friend Graham."

As the child cocked her head and scanned the handsome man from his dusty boots to his black hat, a grin dimpled her cheeks and lit her eyes. "So you're a real cowboy, just like my uncle?"

Graham smiled. "I reckon you could say that, Miss Maddie."

The girl laughed. "Can you say something else cowboy-like?"

"Honey, Mr. Graham isn't here to entertain you." Sasha straightened and turned to the handsome man. "She's a big fan of horses and all things Western."

"Then this visit to the Galloping G should be good for her," Graham said.

Yes, it would definitely do her daughter good. Sasha hoped it would do the same for her. She had some healing to do. She also had a relationship to mend. So why couldn't she seem to turn and walk away from the sexy cowboy who was so good with her daughter?

She glanced toward the barn, where Uncle Roger had disappeared.

"I love horses," Maddie said. "Especially real ones."

Graham chuckled. "A girl after my own heart. Have you ever ridden a *real* one, Maddie?"

"No, not yet. But I have a pretend saddle I put over the back of our sofa at home. And I play like I'm riding that."

Graham glanced at Sasha as if questioning the truth of Maddie's statement.

So she smiled and nodded. "Maddie would ride that towel-draped leather sofa all day if I'd let her."

The little girl lived and breathed horses. And, apparently, she admired the men who worked with them. So, if Sasha wasn't careful, her daughter would pester poor Graham and Uncle Roger to death.

Hoping to defuse what could be an awkward situation, she addressed her daughter. "Mr. Graham has a lot of work to do, honey. And the sooner we let him get back to it, the better."

"That's not a problem," Graham said. "I really don't mind taking a break. In fact, if Maddie wants, I can take her around the Galloping G and show her what a 'real cowboy' does all day, including a broken fence I need to repair."

"That's nice of you," Sasha said, "but it isn't necessary. We just got here and should probably settle in. Besides, Maddie needs to learn a little patience."

"I'll tell you what," Graham said. "While you two unpack, I'll go pick up my mess in that south pasture. When I get back, I can give you that tour." Then he winked at Maddie. "Your mom can come, too."

Sasha probably ought to tell him no. She had a lot to talk over with Uncle Roger. But she couldn't very well have that kind of a heart-to-heart until later this evening, after Maddie went to bed.

For the third time since arriving—or maybe it was the thirty-third—she turned her gaze on Graham, who'd grown an inch or two taller and filled out nicely. He wore a gray T-shirt that didn't mask the muscles in his broad chest. His biceps, which had never been small, now bulged, straining the hem on his short sleeves without any effort on his part.

He still bore the scar on his arm from a riding accident he'd had years ago, a jagged mark left from a barbed-wire fence. But like everything else about him— his hat, his jeans, his smile—he wore the cowboy image well.

She'd always admired Graham and found him attractive in more ways than one. He was—or at least used to be—a straight-up guy. And in spite of the money his family had, there were no pretenses about him, no games. He said what he meant and meant what he said.

Graham was nothing like Gabe, which made him even more appealing now. And that was a good reason for her to steer clear of him. Besides, she was a pregnant single mother. And she'd arrived at the Galloping G with way more baggage than the suitcases she'd brought in the trunk of her car. Certainly way more than a man like Graham would want to deal with. He'd always had a way with the ladies—or at least the girls in high school. So she assumed that he was a free-wheeling bachelor with his pick of willing women.

Yet she found herself nodding in agreement. "Okay, a tour of the ranch sounds fun. While you're going to get your tools and whatnot, Maddie and I will unpack."

Graham lobbed her a crooked grin that nearly stole her breath away. But how could that be? She wasn't a love-struck kid anymore. And she'd experienced far too many of life's realities to even entertain thoughts of ever having a crush—childhood or otherwise—on anyone.

Yet as he turned to walk away, her heart fluttered and her pulse rate spiked, suggesting he still had the ability to send her sense reeling with a simple smile.

By the time Graham returned for his tools in the pasture, the sheriff had come back and stood next to a tow truck, pointing out the SUV that had caused all the damage.

The officer left the driver to his work, then approached Graham. "We'll have that vehicle out of here shortly. The owner has already been informed and has contacted his insurance company."

Graham nodded. "I'm assuming his son was driving?"

"Yep. But from what I understand, the boy lost his license and will be grounded for the rest of the summer."

"I can understand that." Graham could also understand the appeal of an unsupervised teenage party. He'd certainly attended more than his share of those.

But as an adult, he knew the dangers of drinking and driving, no matter what age one was.

After the sheriff left and the tow truck drove out with the SUV, Graham picked up the tools and supplies he'd left in the south pasture and took them to the barn. He hated to leave the repair work on that downed fence unfinished, but he'd do it for Roger. Fortunately, they didn't have any horses grazing out there now. But they would, once his friend Chase Parker delivered them on Friday.

His friend, huh? If that Robinson-Fortune family connection was true, Graham and Chase would be more than friends. They'd actually be related, since Chase was married to Lucie Fortune Chesterfield.

After putting away the tools and supplies, he went in search of Roger and found him leading Lady Jane from the pasture toward the barn.

"What are you doing?" Graham asked. "I thought you'd be inside, talking to Sasha-Marie and getting to know little Maddie."

"I *was* in there. For a while."

"How'd it go?"

"Okay, I guess. Maddie is a little chatterbox, which might prove helpful in piecing together what's going on. She mentioned that her daddy moved out of their house and into an apartment near his work."

"I'm sure that's true. Sasha told me that she and Gabe are separated."

Roger merely nodded as he continued toward the barn, the roan mare walking alongside him.

"What are you doing with Lady Jane?" Graham asked as he followed behind.

"That little girl loves horses, and I figure she'd like to ride a real one instead of her mother's sofa. So I'm going to stable Lady Jane so she'll be closer to the house."

"Good idea." Lady was a gentle mare and would be a good mount for a beginner.

Once they entered the barn, Graham opened the gate of an empty stall. "I assume you and Sasha had a chance to talk."

"Just enough to break the ice some, but not enough to get back on steady ground again."

"I got the feeling that she plans to stay for a while," Graham added.

"Yep." Roger removed the lead from Lady Jane's halter, then closed the gate. "I suspect she came here to lick her wounds, which is fine by me. The Galloping G is the perfect place for her to get back on her feet."

He was right about that. It was at this ranch where Graham and Roger had managed to heal from their terrible loss. And it was here that they hoped to help troubled teenage boys do the same thing.

"You have no idea how happy I am that Sasha-Marie and that jerk finally split up," Roger said. "I knew it was coming. But you'll be glad to know I managed to keep my mouth shut about it."

Graham placed a hand on his old friend's back and grinned. "I'll bet that was tough for a crusty ol' bird who's got a knack for speaking his mind, even when he's not asked."

"You bet it was. And not to toot my own horn, but you'll be glad to know that I didn't break into the 'Hallelujah' chorus when Maddie announced that Gabe moved out of the house."

"Good thing you didn't, Roger. You never could carry a tune."

At that, the old man chuckled. "You're right. My singing would have chased her off for sure."

Graham didn't think so. Sasha had always enjoyed the time she'd spent on the Galloping G. So it didn't surprise him in the least that she would choose to come here to sort out things.

"I wonder what her plans are," Graham said. "Hopefully, Gabe is paying her child support."

Roger blew out a raspberry. "I wouldn't be surprised if, once that guy hit the road, he never looked back. And if he didn't, it'd be okay by me. Gabe Smith was bad news, wrapped in a shiny wrapper. But Sasha doesn't need the likes of him. Not with me around, anyway. I'll look out for her. Besides, she has a college degree. I suspect she could put that to good use."

"There's time to ask her about that later," Graham

said. "For now, you ought to enjoy the time you have with her."

"Yep, I intend to. In the meantime, I'm going to go inside and fix dinner. I'd planned to make meat loaf and baked potatoes this evening. S'pose I still will. But if I'd known Sasha-Marie and Maddie were coming, I would have taken steaks out of the freezer. It seems like we have a lot to celebrate."

Maybe Roger did. But something told Graham that Sasha wasn't nearly as happy about the split as her uncle was.

"You might not want to make such a big deal out of it," Graham said. "She married the guy and undoubtedly loved him. She probably doesn't feel like celebrating."

"I wasn't talking about making a big whoopty-do that he was out of her life, although I'd sure as heck raise my glass to that. But I'm glad she's back at the ranch. I've missed her. And I've regretted not having a chance to get to know little Maddie. She's a cutie pie, isn't she?"

Yes, she was, at that. "She sure looks a lot like her mama."

"You got that right. And she's just as spunky, too."

Before Graham could agree, Sasha and Maddie stepped out on the big, wraparound porch.

"Looks like it's time for the tour to begin," Graham said quietly to Roger. "If she wasn't expecting, I'd suggest we take horses, which would no doubt please Maddie. But I think we should take the Gator."

"Good idea. I've delivered my share of foals and calves, but I don't know squat about bringing a human baby into the world."

Just the thought of Sasha delivering at the ranch and not in a state-of-the-art medical facility twisted Graham's gut into a double knot. He'd better suggest she find a doctor in Austin—and quickly. From the size of her baby bump, she'd need a good one soon.

Yet even the fact that she was expecting didn't take away from her beauty. How had he missed the corn-silk color of her hair before—or those expressive blue eyes?

"We're ready for that tour when you are," she said, as she and her pretty Mini-Me daughter stepped off the porch.

Sasha walked slowly, but Maddie marched right up to her uncle. "Are you going with us, Uncle Roger? Are you going to show us all your horses?"

Roger blessed the child with a smile and cupped her cheek with his liver-spotted, work-roughened hand. "Not this time, sweetie. I'm going to cook our dinner. But don't worry. Graham will give you a good tour—and probably a better one than I could."

The child looked at Graham with hope-filled eyes—their pretty color reminded him of a field of bluebonnets, blowing in the breeze. "Do you know where my uncle keeps his horses?"

"Actually, we only have a few right now. But come this weekend, you'll see five more of them grazing in the south forty."

Maddie's eyes widened. "A whole *herd*?"

Graham couldn't help appreciating her enthusiasm. "Well, it's not exactly a herd, at least, not a big one. We'll have our hands full with those five for now."

He'd thought his answer would appease her, but apparently, one of her questions merely led to another. "Where are you going to get them?" she asked. "Do you have to ride into the mountains and desert and wilderness to find them?"

Graham bit back a chuckle. "My friend Chase Parker has rescue horses already on his ranch. He's going to deliver them to us."

"I can't wait to see them," she said.

"Then I'll make sure you're around when they arrive. In the meantime, let's go check out the ranch." Graham glanced at Sasha and nodded toward the barn. "Come on. We'll take the Gator."

"You got *gators* in Texas?" Maddie asked, struggling to match his strides. "Do they bite?"

Graham smiled. "We don't have any alligators on the Galloping G. I was actually talking about our off-road utility vehicle."

He led them to the rear of the barn, where he'd left the Gator parked. Once he helped Maddie into the backseat and secured her with a seat belt, something the previous owner had installed, he and Sasha climbed into the front. Then he started the engine.

What a turn this day had taken. Graham's morning had started out in the usual way—a shower before downing coffee and the biscuits and gravy Roger had made for them. Then he'd ridden out to check on the pasture where they planned to keep the new horses.

When he'd spotted the damage to the fence, as well as the battered front end of the Cadillac Escalade that had been left in the pasture, wheel wells deep in the mud, he'd realized things weren't going to be as usual today.

But nothing had prepared him for Sasha and Maddie's arrival a few hours later, which ensured that, at least for the time being, things on the Galloping G would be far from ordinary.

He just hoped the changes would be good ones.

While Graham appeared to be doing his best to avoid any big potholes on the dirt road on which they'd been driving, the Gator made a quick swerve, causing Sasha to grab the dashboard and brace herself. She turned and looked over her shoulder. "Are you okay, Maddie?"

"Yep." The seven-year-old patted her seat belt and flashed a bright-eyed smile that revealed her missing tooth. "I'm all buckled in."

"Sorry about that," Graham said. "We had a heavy rain a couple days ago, and it left the road a mess."

"I remember the summer storms we used to have," Sasha said. "I actually thought they were cool."

The rumbles of thunder and the lightning that tore across the sky had been an amazing, celestial light show. Some people were frightened by the sights and sounds, especially when they struck at night. But Sasha hadn't been one of them. And she doubted Maddie would be, either.

Graham swung around a mud puddle. "Are the bumps and turns too jarring for you?" He nodded toward her belly.

Sasha cast a reassuring smile his way. "No, I'm doing

okay. And believe it or not, the baby seems to be enjoying it as much as Maddie is."

"Apparently, she takes after her mom in more than just her looks." Graham tossed her a boyish grin. "You always were a tomboy who tried to convince Peter and me that you were as tough and strong as horseshoes."

She responded with the title of a song. "Anything you can do…"

Graham laughed. "You used to sing that to us all the time."

That was true. She'd taunted them with the lively tune from *Annie Get Your Gun* every chance she got.

Sasha had never seen the actual musical on Broadway, or anywhere else for that matter. But one summer day, when she was visiting, Uncle Roger had taken them all to see a local talent show. She'd loved the performance by a high school girl and boy who'd sung that song.

"That's too funny," Graham said. "I'd nearly forgotten it."

Singing it to Graham had been one of her many ploys to get his attention, although it hadn't worked.

However, it did seem to catch his interest now.

Graham turned to the right, following a narrow road, and pointed to a grassy area. "This is the stretch of broken fence I've been fixing. I'll need to get it done soon because we plan to keep some of the rescue horses here."

Maddie let out a little gasp. "Can we come back again and see it? After the horses get here?"

"Sure." Graham shot a questioning look at Sasha. "That is, if your mom doesn't mind."

"No, of course not. Maddie would love to see them grazing in the field." Sasha's warm smile shot clean through Graham, setting off a spark in his chest.

He'd only meant to make Maddie happy, but the fact that Sasha realized he had a soft spot for her daughter and that she was so clearly pleased by it, caught him off guard. It also left him a little unbalanced, since he hadn't meant to earn her praise.

As a result, he decided to end the tour for today and head back. Several quiet minutes later, he parked the Gator on the side of the barn.

"What's that?" Sasha pointed to the concrete foundation they'd had poured last week. "Is Uncle Roger building something, maybe a new barn?"

"That's going to be the new bunkhouse. We were going to remodel the old one, but after we got started, we realized it was in bad shape and wouldn't meet code. So we decided to start from scratch. We also built a couple of cabins for the boys."

Her brow furrowed. "The *boys*?"

Apparently, Roger hadn't mentioned their plan to her.

"Horses aren't all we hope to rescue," Graham said. "We're going to take in some troubled teenagers and put them to work gentling the horses, something we hope will give them a new perspective on life."

Her eyes widened, and her lips parted. "Seriously? That's a great plan. And very admirable."

Graham probably should have let Roger tell her about it, since her uncle needed to score a few points. But what was done was done, so he shrugged. "The idea started out as a tribute to Peter, but then it sort of took on a spin of its own. We've already talked to the school board, as well as the juvenile probation department."

"Taking in those boys won't be easy," Sasha said. "And even though you guys should be able to relate well, there will be a ton of paperwork and regulations."

"Yes, we know." And Graham already had that covered. "As a side note," he added with a grin, "you weren't the only one who went to college."

"That's right." She returned his smile. "I forgot."

As much as he liked living on the Galloping G, and as much as he loved helping Roger, he had a bigger goal in life than just working on someone else's ranch.

"What was your major?" she asked.

"Business." He'd actually earned an MBA. "So I have it all worked out."

"I'd always assumed you'd eventually go to work for your dad."

"No, I'd never do that." He'd dreamed of having a business of his own someday, one that didn't have anything to do with Robinson Tech. In fact, even though everyone, especially his father and his siblings, had expected him to join them at the corporate offices after his graduation, Graham had refused.

There was no way he could ever work with his old man. He and Gerald Robinson might have buried the hatchet in some ways over the past couple of years, but Graham still resented his father's my-way-or-the-highway attitude.

Besides, he felt good about the nonprofit organization he and Roger were creating. And he planned to use his education and his connections to make it all happen just as they planned.

"Mommy," Maddie said. "Can I go in the kitchen and find Uncle Roger? He might want my help fixing dinner."

Sasha laughed. "Sure, honey. Go ahead. I'll be there in a minute."

When the little girl hurried toward the front porch, Sasha said, "Tell me more about this idea of yours. It's not that I'm trying to dissuade you. I think it's noble. But it's… Well, it just surprises me, that's all."

Graham had a feeling it wasn't just the idea that surprised her. It was the fact that he was still living here, eight years later. Some guys might be offended by that, but he liked being able to still pull her chain and tease her a bit. "I guess there's more to me than met your eye, huh?"

For a moment, their gazes met and locked. He expected her to comment, to tease him, to… He wasn't sure what was swirling around behind those pretty blue eyes.

Instead she let his comment go.

"Where did you come up with that plan?" she asked.

"Peter and I both had wild streaks. I'd like to think that we would have settled down in time, but I'm not sure that's true. I was pretty rebellious back in the day."

"I never understood why. The way I saw it, you had everything a kid could ever want."

Graham could neither agree nor disagree with her. It wasn't that he'd had an unhappy childhood. His father had supplied his family with everything they could possibly ask for, other than his time, of course. Gerald Robinson, or rather, Jerome Fortune—damn, would Graham ever get used to that name?—had always seemed to be at the office or away on a business trip. And while he supplied his children with plenty of material possessions, he'd held back on his affection. That in and of itself would cause plenty of kids to rebel. But Graham had other reasons for the issues between him and his dad. Things he'd never told anyone and certainly wouldn't share with Sasha.

"Maybe I was a born rebel," he said.

"Peter, too?" She slowly shook her head, not believing him. But her cousin had a wild side, too, even if she hadn't been aware of it.

Graham and Peter had met in middle school and become best friends. They were both energetic and creative, often getting in trouble in class—and partying on the weekends.

Roger had always taken their rowdy behavior with a grain of salt, saying boys would be boys. But Graham's dad considered it outright rebellion, especially when he knew Graham was probably his brightest child and had such unrealized potential.

"I guess you could say I sometimes led Peter astray," Graham said, although that really wasn't true. Still, he wasn't about to let the conversation continue on that same thread and open up any more than he'd already done.

Since Sasha remained seated in the Gator, apparently eager to hear more, he opted to change the subject.

"How long are you planning to be here?" he asked.

"I don't know. For the near future, I suppose. And until I can figure out my next step."

"Well, for however long it is, I'm glad you came back and that you brought Maddie. It'll be good for Roger."

He'd meant his comment to give her some peace, but her gaze nearly drilled a hole right through him. She seemed to be asking him something with her eyes, but he'd be damned if he knew what it was.

Chapter Three

Graham was right. Sasha's visit to the Galloping G might prove to be good for Roger. It would definitely be good for her and Maddie.

But what about you? she was tempted to ask Graham. *How do you feel about my return?*

A moment after the question rose in her mind, she shook the dust and cobwebs from it. Those days of carefree, youthful dreams were long gone, even if Graham was even more handsome, more appealing than ever.

Besides, even when life had been innocent and simple, that silly crush she'd had on him was hopeless. He'd never considered her anything other than a pesky kid. In fact, the last time she'd seen him on the Galloping G, when he'd come by to tell her uncle goodbye before he left for college, he'd called her "Sassy Pants" and had tugged on the ponytail she wore.

But then again, she'd only been fifteen at the time. She'd also been a late bloomer and had looked young for her age. Actually, she still did. Even though she was nearing the ripe old age of thirty, people often mistook her for Maddie's babysitter.

Trying to rein in her wild and inappropriate thoughts, Sasha thanked him for the tour. "Maddie really enjoyed it. And so did I."

"You're welcome. It was my pleasure. When Chase brings those horses on Friday, I'll give you a better explanation of our rescue operation."

She nodded but didn't make any attempt to get out of the Gator. She still had something weighing on her mind, a comment she'd made and the apology she owed him for it. "I'm sorry if I made it sound as though I didn't think you and Uncle Roger could handle running a home for wayward teenagers. Or that you didn't have legalities and logistics all planned out. I'm sure you do. I was just surprised to hear it, that's all."

Graham, his left wrist perched on top of the steering wheel, his right on the gearshift, studied her for a moment. As he did, their gazes held steady.

"No offense taken," he said. "You always have been one to speak your mind. And for the record, your uncle isn't the only one who's glad you're back."

Her heart warmed at his words. It had been a long time since she'd felt wanted or appreciated. Gabe certainly hadn't made her feel that way in the past few years. In fact, he never really had. "Thanks for saying that, Graham. Whether it's true or not, I appreciate hearing it."

"It wasn't just fluff to make you feel good, Sassy Pants."

She smiled at the nickname that had once driven her crazy. But today it flowed from his lips like an endearment.

Or maybe she was so starved for affection and validation that she would latch on to almost anything she could construe as a compliment. But whose fault was that? She only had herself to blame for remaining in a relationship that had fizzled out years ago.

In fact, in retrospect, her marriage had begun to unravel from the day she and Gabe returned from their honeymoon.

Sure, she'd thought that she'd loved him at the time and that he'd felt the same way about her. But the dream she'd once harbored, to finally have a home and family of her own, soon ended, and reality had set in as soon as the wedding-day sparkle was gone.

Tears welled in her eyes once again, and she blinked them back. But she wasn't doing a very good job of it.

"What's the matter?" Graham asked. "Are you okay?"

The last thing she wanted him to think was that she felt sorry for herself, when it was more her concern about raising her children without a father. The girls needed a loving, male influence in their lives. So she forced a smile to go along with the explanation she hoped he'd believe. "I'm fine. Just a few happy tears overflowing. It feels so good to be back on the Galloping G."

And it really did. But that didn't mean she wasn't grieving for the happy family she'd once thought she'd have.

She sniffled, then proceeded to climb from the Gator. "I'd better go inside and check on Maddie. She's probably driving poor Uncle Roger crazy."

"I'm sure he's fine."

She suspected that was true, but she couldn't stay outside with Graham forever, wishing things were different than they really were.

"Will we see you at dinner?" she asked.

"I usually eat most of my meals in the ranch house. Your uncle is one heck of a cook. So yeah. I'll be there."

She nodded, then turned away, leaving Graham seated in the Gator.

As she headed to the back door that led to the kitchen, she took a big breath, relishing the country air and the whinny of a horse in the pasture.

Yes, it was good to be back. While she was here, maybe she'd come up with a feasible game plan for the future. She had a degree in social work and might as well put it to good use.

But what about the cost of infant day care? Gabe had said he'd send additional money for that, but she wasn't sure she could depend upon him to carry through with it. But at least she'd get a decent amount of child support, which was one of the details they'd agreed upon when they filed for divorce. So she was right back to her most troubling dilemma.

She'd never intended to be a single mother, but life didn't always turn out the way a person expected it to.

Nevertheless, she would create a new family with her daughters—minus a daddy, of course.

She had no other choice. Her children's happiness depended upon it.

Uncle Roger, who'd been a cook in the navy years ago, outdid himself at dinner this evening. Or maybe Sasha felt that way because she'd missed sharing meals with him on the ranch.

After the first couple of bites, Sasha said, "I'd like to have your recipe for this meat loaf. Grandma Dixon used to make it, but she always covered hers with a weird mushroom sauce. I like your version much better. It doesn't need anything on top, other than some good, old-fashioned ketchup."

"I'll try to write something down for you," her uncle said. "But I'm not sure how to go about it. I just throw things together."

"Then you have a good sense about how something is supposed to taste. You're an awesome cook."

Uncle Roger beamed, his bright-eyed smile shaving years off his face. "Thanks, Sasha-Marie."

But it wasn't just the main dish that Sasha found remarkable. "I haven't had baked potatoes with all the fixings in ages." She pointed to the small bowls of toppings he'd set out on the table. "Butter, fresh chives, sour cream, grated cheddar, real bacon… You didn't skimp on anything."

When her uncle didn't respond, she looked up from

her plate to see him and Graham shooting glances at each other. She tried to read their expressions, to no avail.

Had they, over the years, created a silent language of their own? Then again, there was still a lot left to be said this evening, plus a hatchet to be buried. And they all knew it. Well, the adults did. Little Maddie was eating away, oblivious of the tension that still stretched between Sasha and Roger.

"Thanks for going to all this trouble for me," she said. "It's a perfect welcome-home meal."

At that, Uncle Roger broke into another grin. "I'm glad you're here, honey."

"Me, too," she admitted. And she was grateful that, in spite of the fact that he'd been hurt, he'd opened his arms and heart to her once again, just as he'd done after her parents died.

She speared her fork into a crunchy piece of romaine lettuce, as well as a plump chunk of tomato that had obviously come fresh from the vine. But she hadn't been prepared for the familiar taste of the vinaigrette. "Oh, my gosh. You even made Aunt Helen's salad dressing. Now I'm really impressed."

Roger's tired blue eyes lit up and he winked. "That was my way of having her here with us tonight."

"What a nice thought."

After they finished dinner, Roger brought out dessert: chocolate-chip ice cream and store-bought peanut butter cookies.

"I like ranch food," Maddie said. "It's really good."

Roger, whose smile stretched from ear to ear, said,

"You just wait for breakfast. I'll make silver-dollar pancakes for you."

The man had always been a whiz in the kitchen, going out of his way to make sure he pleased those sharing his table. And while Sasha should volunteer to do the dishes herself and give him a much-deserved break this evening, they still had things to discuss. And they needed to do that in private.

"I'll help you with the dishes," she told her uncle.

"That's not necessary. I clean up as I go."

"Yes, I know. But I'd like to talk to you."

As Roger nodded in agreement, Graham spoke up. "That sounds like a good plan to me." Then he turned his attention to Maddie. "Since you and I are off the hook for cleanup detail, let's go into the living room, kick back and watch the sports channel."

Maddie wrinkled her nose. "But I don't like sports. Don't you want to watch Disney or Nickelodeon or cartoons instead?"

Graham sat back in his chair, crossed his arms over his chest and scrunched his own face. "What do you mean, you don't like *sports*? Not even pro rodeo?"

Maddie sat up, her eyes brightening. "I thought sports meant football and basketball and dumb ol' golf. But I'd like to watch rodeo stuff."

"Something told me you would be okay with that." Graham glanced at Sasha and winked in camaraderie, setting off a warm flutter in her heart. She doubted he had any idea how that small, brief connection had affected her, just as he hadn't in the past, because he turned back to her daughter. "I'll make you a deal, Maddie. If we can't find any rodeo on TV, then I'll let you be in charge of the remote."

The child clapped her hands. "Deal!"

"Then what are we waiting for?" Graham pushed back his chair and stood. "Let's get out of here before they put you and me to work."

Maddie slid off her seat, then followed the handsome cowboy into the family room, leaving Sasha and Uncle Roger alone.

As her uncle began to clear the table, she said, "I owe you an apology."

He merely looked at her, waiting for her to explain.

"You tried to warn me about Gabe, and I should have listened. But I was young and headstrong back then. I was also in love with the idea of marriage."

"Yeah, well, I knew that no-good son of a…" Roger cleared his throat, pausing as if trying to temper his response. Then he blew out a heavy sigh. "Well, that's all muddy water under a rickety old bridge to nowhere."

"Yes, I know. But it needs to be said, just the same." She picked up the plates, bowls and silverware, while he grabbed the glasses.

"I s'pose you're right about that. But just so you know, when I was that age and had fallen for your aunt, I wouldn't have let anyone talk me out of marrying her. So I can't blame you for not listening to me."

"I'm glad you understand, but that isn't the only reason I need to apologize."

He arched a gray, bushy eyebrow.

"I'm sorry for not keeping in better contact with you. I should have done that." She stacked the dirty dishes on the counter near the sink, then took the glasses from him and set them down, too. "It wouldn't have hurt me to visit some and call you more often."

"Yeah, well..." Roger paused again, his craggy brow creased as if he was wading through his thoughts and feelings. Then he shrugged. "The phone line goes both ways. Besides, the fault is probably mine. I shouldn't have stirred things up at your wedding."

"I knew something happened that day, but I wasn't sure what. You were so quiet and grim." She reached into the cupboard under the sink for the bottle of dish soap. "And Gabe was... Well, he was as tense as a fence post and angry about something."

"Gabe and I had words," Roger said. "And I damn near beat the crap out of him. The best man and the groomsmen had to pull me off him. So I'm sorry about that." He chuckled. "Actually, I'm mostly sorry someone interfered before I had a chance to let him have it. I would have enjoyed giving him a black eye, a fat lip and a bloody nose. But it's just as well. If I had, it would have ruined your special day."

She laughed, imagining a battered groom standing at the altar. "You're right. I wouldn't have been happy about that."

"Either way, honey, I should have held my tongue. And my temper."

It wasn't like her uncle to get into brawls, especially at a church and dressed in a tuxedo. "What made you want to fight him?"

"The stuff he said to me. Things meant to rile me up, I 'spect." Again he shrugged as if it no longer mattered.

But it did matter, especially if they wanted to put it all behind them.

"What did he say to you?" she asked.

Roger pondered her question for the longest time. When she thought he might never answer, he said, "I wanted to have a talk with him before the ceremony. I figured, with your daddy and your grandpa gone, that job was up to me. So I found him and his friends waiting for the ceremony to start in one of the small rooms at the church. They were already dressed and throwing back shots of whiskey as if the bachelor party had never ended."

She'd smelled alcohol on Gabe's breath, tasted it, too. She'd assumed he'd been nervous and had wanted to take the edge off.

"Now, I'll admit," Roger said, "I ain't a teetotaler. But I didn't think the preacher or the Good Lord would have appreciated those boys tying one on at the church on a Saturday morning. And I told 'em so. But Gabe didn't take to being scolded. I should have taken the hint then, but I decided to try a different approach and asked if I could talk to him alone."

"When you spoke in private, what did he say?"

"Actually, he told me there wasn't anything I had to say that his buddies couldn't hear."

"Gabe could get pretty mouthy when he drank," Sasha admitted. "Especially when he was with his friends." One part of her didn't want to hear the details, but she needed to know. "So, then what happened?"

"I just told him to be good to you, to respect you. And then I said, if he didn't, he'd have to answer to me."

She wouldn't have expected any less from her uncle. Roger Gibault might be a bit gruff and rough around the edges, but he had a good heart. And he was respectful to women.

"Apparently, Gabe took offense at what I said and considered it a threat." Roger turned on the spigot, letting warm water flow into the sink. He squeezed a squirt of dish soap under the flow, then chuckled. "Hell, it *was* a threat. And he didn't like it."

When the water and bubbles reached the proper level, Sasha shut off the faucet. "Gabe never listened to his father, either. He didn't like being told what to do."

"That doesn't surprise me. It didn't take me but five minutes to realize he thought he was pretty damn special. And that he was a big-mouthed rabble-rouser. But I hadn't realized he was such an ass. If I had, I would have seen it coming."

"Seen what coming?"

"Gabe gave me a shove that sent me flying against the wall and damn near shook the church rafters. I hit it so hard I got an egg on the back of my head. Hell, the thud alone knocked a framed picture of the Good Shepherd onto the floor."

"Oh, my gosh. I hope he apologized."

"Nope. It didn't faze him. Instead he opened his yap and lit my fuse."

Sasha hadn't realized that their words had progressed to violence. "What did he say?"

"You want a direct quote?"

She nodded, bracing herself. "Yes, please tell me."

Roger's eyes narrowed to a glare, and his voice deepened, the tone chilly. "'Who do you think you are, old man? You aren't anything to me. And just so you know, I've got your little Sasha-Marie right where I want her—in my bed and under my thumb. So keep your mouth shut and don't even try interfering in our lives, or I'll make sure you never see her again.'"

Sasha cringed. Had she known this on her wedding day, she might have…done what? Told Gabe that the wedding was off?

No, sadly, she might not have wanted to believe the worst about him. She'd been so starry-eyed and hope-filled that day. But now, eight years later, she realized what Roger was telling her was true.

"I wanted to knock him down to size," Roger said. "So when I got my balance, I doubled up my fist and went after him. I landed a pretty good one on his chin, although I'd been aiming for his nose. He might have thought of me as just an old man, but I'm cowboy strong. And I would have beaten the crap out of him then and there, if his friends hadn't pulled me off him."

"I'm sorry, Uncle Roger. I had no idea what a mean, selfish jerk Gabe was."

"Well, what's done is done. After it was all over, I realized how embarrassed you would have been if I'd battered your groom until he was black and blue."

She smiled. "I almost wish you'd done it now."

He chuckled. "Me, too. But my mama and daddy taught me better than that. I just wish my temper didn't sometimes get the best of me."

She smiled and opened her arms. "Can I give you a hug?"

"You betcha." He stepped into the embrace, and they held each other close. That is, until the baby shifted and gave her a quick jab with either a little foot or fist.

"Well, I'll be damned." Roger dropped his arms, took a step back and looked down at her expanded belly. "I guess I'm not the only one in the family with a feisty side and a protective streak. That little one has a good kick."

"She's strong, that's for sure. And she's always making her presence known."

"Well, I'm looking forward to meeting her. I wish I could have seen more of Maddie when she was a baby. But…" He clamped his mouth shut and slowly shook his head.

"You came to see her when she was born. Then you left quickly. Did Gabe chase you off?"

"He didn't actually say anything too bad that time. Maybe because there hadn't been any alcohol involved and he didn't have an army of friends surrounding him. But each time I glanced at him, he glared at me, so I decided to end my visit and to stay away. I didn't want to avoid you, but I knew if I came around more often, things might eventually blow up again. Besides, I figured my presence alone would upset your husband and he might take it out on you."

"So you made that sacrifice for me?"

"That's what you do when you love someone, Sasha-Marie."

She placed a hand on his arm, fingering the softness of his worn flannel shirt. "I hope you know how much I love and appreciate you."

Roger's eyes glistened and his grin deepened. The hard feelings he'd once harbored had clearly softened.

He might have said that his anger had been directed at Gabe, but she suspected that he'd resented her for not listening to him in the first place, for not calling him regularly or visiting on occasion.

But he was right. That was all water under the bridge now.

"I'd better check on Maddie," she said. "She's liable to pester Graham more than I ever did."

Roger laughed. "You were a pistol when you were a youngster, that's a fact."

Sasha smiled at the truth. She might have been a little headstrong, but she'd also had a loving heart, just like Maddie, who shared the same vivacious energy. Thank goodness her daughter hadn't picked up any of Gabe's bad traits.

Instead Maddie resembled Sasha in so many ways, and not just because of their big blue eyes and fair hair.

As Sasha entered the living room, where she assumed Maddie and Graham were watching television, she expected the cowboy to jump up immediately, glad for her return and a chance to escape the precocious child.

But she hadn't been prepared for the sight that met her eyes. The two were seated on the floor, side by side. Maddie's crayons and coloring books were spread upon the coffee table. Seeing the two of them working—or rather, playing—together was enough to turn Sasha's heart inside out.

"Well, I'll be darned," Roger said. "I never would

have guessed it, son, but you make one heck of a baby-sitter."

Graham glanced up, a boyish grin stretched across his face. "I might be having a good time, but I'm not for hire. So don't get any ideas."

Unfortunately, Sasha was getting plenty of them. And they didn't have anything to do with hiring Graham to watch her children. But she couldn't afford to let that old childish crush get out of hand, especially when she knew her feelings would always be one-sided.

As a waning moon shone overhead that night, lighting the familiar path, Graham headed toward his cabin. He'd stayed at the big house long enough to see that Sasha and Roger had gotten things settled between them.

He was glad about that. He'd have to ask his old friend to share the details tomorrow during morning chores.

In return, Graham would have some things to tell Roger, too. While coloring with Maddie this evening, he'd gotten an earful. The girl was not only a cutie pie, but she was talkative to boot.

Sasha would probably flip out if she knew Maddie had filled him in on some of their family secrets. Not that she'd come right out and told him anything point blank, but Graham was pretty good at connecting dots and asking a few carefully constructed questions now and then.

From what he'd gathered, Gabe had traveled on business and was rarely home. But whenever he was around,

Maddie had to keep quiet and play in her room. *Shh!* her mama would tell her. *Daddy's tired, and you know how cranky he can get.*

"Was it hard to keep quiet?" Graham had asked the girl.

"No, because then Mama and I would leave. Sometimes we'd get groceries or go to the park. But we always got ice cream or a snack on the way home."

"Sounds like, in some ways, it was fun when he came home."

"Not always," she said. "Not when he yelled at me or Mama."

Graham had never met the man Sasha married, but he hadn't needed to. Roger was a good judge of character. And now little Maddie had added her own spin on what life with Gabe Smith was like.

As Graham reached the front stoop of his cabin, he stopped and turned, scanning the ranch that would soon be known as Peter's Place. He suspected Peter would have been proud of their plan.

As he turned back to reach for doorknob, his cell phone rang. He pulled it from his pocket and glanced at the lit screen. He didn't recognize the number, but he answered anyway.

"Mr. Gibault?" a man asked.

"No, this is Graham Robinson."

"Oh. Yeah. Sorry, I got my names and numbers confused. Anyway, this is Brad Taylor with the juvenile probation department. I have a young man I'd like to bring out to the Galloping G tomorrow. He's already passed the screening process. Are you ready for him?"

The bunkhouse wasn't finished, but they had a new two-bedroom cabin into which the boy could move. Graham also planned to hire a full-time counselor, as well as a teacher, since most of the boys would be lacking school credits. He and Roger had interviewed several applicants already, but they hadn't made any decisions yet. Of course, that was going to be a top priority now.

Still, he said, "Sure, we're ready for him."

"Good. Then we'll see you tomorrow. I'll email a copy of his file, as well as the psychological evaluation, so you can read them over before we arrive. Look for us after one o'clock."

"Thanks." Graham couldn't wait to tell Roger they would soon see their plan coming together.

After Mr. Taylor ended the call, Graham made one last scan of the ranch and noticed that Sasha had walked outside the main house and now stood on the wraparound porch. She didn't venture any farther than that. She just gripped the railing and looked out into the night, same as he'd done earlier.

Graham slipped the cell back into his jeans pocket. All the while, he watched Sasha, saw her wander over to the porch swing, then take a seat and set the thing in motion.

He wondered what she had on her mind. When she'd been a kid, she used to sit outside all the time, especially in the evenings. He asked her about it once, teasing her while he did. *What're you doing, Sassy Pants? Mooning over a boy?*

Maybe.

Does he know you like him?

At that, she'd let out a wobbly sigh. *I wish. But he doesn't even know I'm alive.*

The summer before Graham left for college, she'd sat out there night after night. He'd always assumed she was daydreaming about the boy she was sweet on.

Was that what she was doing now? Thinking about Gabe? Wondering if he'd come looking for her? Plotting some way to win him back?

As much as he hoped she was smarter than that, she was pregnant with Gabe's baby. So it made sense that she might want to hold things together.

Graham was sorely tempted to cross the yard and tell her she was better off without him. He could also assure her that he'd look out for her until she got back on her feet.

But what made him think she'd appreciate an offer like that? It wasn't as if she was mooning over *him*.

Too bad, he thought. For some totally illogical reason, a part of him wished that she were.

Chapter Four

Around one o'clock on Friday afternoon, Graham went to the barn to repair a broken hinge on one of the stalls. Chase had called earlier to say that he would be bringing the horses later today, but not all of them would be ready to be turned out to pasture or into one of the corrals. One might need to be stabled.

Graham had just tightened a loose bolt when he heard a car pull into the yard. He suspected it was the probation officer bringing their first teenage resident, but there was no way to know for sure unless he went outside. So he left his tools resting on a bale of straw and strode out of the barn and into the yard.

A white sedan with government license plates and a stoical teenager sitting in the passenger seat told Graham his assumption had been right.

The man behind the wheel had to be Brad Taylor, who'd asked if Graham and Roger were ready for their first kid to arrive. But ready or not, it was showtime.

When a red-haired man in his early forties climbed out of the sedan, Graham introduced himself and greeted him with a firm handshake.

"It's nice to meet you," Taylor said. "My supervisor said that you were highly recommended by the references you provided."

"I'm glad to hear that. I told you we were prepared to take in kids, and we are. But for the record, the teacher we just hired won't be able to start until next Monday."

"No problem." Taylor placed his hands in the pockets of his khaki slacks. "Jonah's behind on some of his credits, but he ought to catch up quickly if he's working one-on-one with an instructor."

"I hope so," Graham said. "In the meantime, he'll be able to settle in and get used to the way we do things around here."

"Thanks for providing a place for him," Taylor said. "He's not thrilled about coming here, but like I told you on the phone, his options were limited."

The email report had provided Graham with the kid's background, as well as the trouble he'd gotten into.

Jonah Wright came from a broken home. His dad had run off a couple of years ago, leaving the mother to raise Jonah and three younger children. The man didn't pay her any child support, so that forced her to work two jobs to make ends meet. She needed help and cooperation from all the kids, especially the oldest. But instead of taking on more family responsibility, Jonah started acting out and ditching school. His mother was at her wit's end. And when he was caught stealing a camera from the photography classroom at his high school, she feared he would lead her other children astray if he didn't straighten up.

Then, when a recent shoplifting violation at a department store resulted in Jonah's arrest and prosecution, she'd poured out her frustration to the court. At that point, Brad Taylor had stepped in and suggested the boy be placed on a working ranch to help him get his priorities in order. And that led to Jonah becoming the very first teenage resident of Peter's Place.

It wasn't until Brad opened the passenger door that Jonah slid out of the vehicle, wearing a black T-shirt with a white skull and crossbones on the front and a pair of pants that rode so low on his hips that, if he sneezed, they'd probably slip to his knees. His beat-up black sneakers were untied, the floppy laces frayed and dirty from being stepped on.

His very appearance screamed rebellion, and the scowl on his face suggested he wore a chip on his shoulder.

Graham reached out a hand, giving the teen a man's welcome. "I'm glad you're here. We have some rescue horses arriving in a couple of hours, and we'll need all the help we can get."

"I don't know squat about horses or cattle," Jonah said. "So if you're looking for a cowboy, you're out of luck."

Roger, who'd just come out of the house, approached just in time to hear the boy's comment. But like the loving, slow-to-react father he'd been to Peter, he glossed over the kid's attitude and appearance—something Graham had always liked and admired about him. Not that Roger hadn't given Peter and Graham hell at times, but he'd chosen his battles wisely.

"It ain't that hard to learn," the elderly rancher said. "You'll get the hang of it in no time at all, son."

The boy merely clicked his tongue, rolled his eyes and looked away.

Brad pulled the car keys from his pocket. "I'll be back in a few days to check up on you, Jonah."

The kid made another tongue click. "Whatever."

"Actually," Brad said, turning to Graham and Roger, "it might be sooner than that. I have another boy who's going to need placement. I'll know for sure after court next week, so I'll be in touch."

Graham shook his hand. "Like I said, we have room for six right now. And once the bunkhouse is finished next month and we've hired additional staff, we can add twenty more."

Brad nodded, then climbed back into his car. After he drove off, Sasha came outside and made her way to the new arrival.

Apparently, she wanted to meet Jonah, too. But Graham couldn't blame her for that. She was a mother and probably wanted to get a feel for the young stranger who was going to be living on the ranch.

"Hi there." She reached out a hand to greet Jonah. "I'm Sasha. My daughter and I are staying here, too."

The kid studied her outstretched hand for a beat,

then took it, albeit reluctantly. "You and your kid get in trouble?"

Sasha smiled. "I've made some bad choices in my life, but I plan to do things differently from here on out. And coming to Peter's Place is going to help me do that. I hope you feel the same way soon."

He shrugged. But his expression seemed to have softened a bit, just being around Sasha.

Hell, just being around her had caused Graham to rethink a few things, too. That glossy, white-blond hair that tumbled over her shoulders, those expressive blue eyes, the alluring scent of ripe peaches...

Don't forget, his better judgment countered, *she's also carrying another man's baby.*

"I hope you like spaghetti," Sasha said to Jonah. "My daughter and I are fixing dinner tonight."

"It's okay, but I like pizza a lot better."

Graham wanted to roll his eyes at the kid's attitude, but only when it was directed at Sasha. Instead he kept himself in check.

"Jonah," Roger said, "we'll show you where you'll be staying. Get your bag and come with us."

The boy grabbed the small canvas tote that held his belongings, then followed the men to the newly built two-bedroom cabin, which was only fifty yards from the older but similar structure in which Graham lived.

"Since you're the first one to move in," Roger said, "you have your choice of bedrooms and bunks."

Jonah scanned the small, ten-by-twelve living area, with its bookshelf, love seat and two chairs. "Where's the TV?"

"There isn't one," Roger said. "But you won't be spending much time in here, other than for sleep. If you need to entertain yourself, you'll find plenty of good books—like *Moby Dick*, which was always a favorite of mine."

There went another eye roll, followed by a tongue click. "How am I s'posed to play the video games I brought?"

"I'm afraid you won't be able to." Graham smiled. "But like Roger said, you won't miss playing them while you're in the cabin. You'll be too eager to get a good night's sleep."

The boy's jaw dropped.

"Breakfast is in the big house at six a.m.," Roger added. "If you're late, we don't eat lunch until noon. So I suggest you set the alarm."

Jonah, whose droopy britches revealed more than just the waistband of his red boxer shorts, shook his head. "Man, it's summer vacation. Didn't anyone tell you guys that it's okay to sleep in?"

"Not on the Galloping G, it ain't." Roger nodded to one of the two bedrooms. "Put your gear away, then come outside with us. We'll show you around and give you a list of chores."

Jonah let out an expletive, followed by a grumble.

Graham had told Brad Taylor that he and Roger were ready for that first kid. He just hoped that was true.

It was nearly four o'clock when Chase Parker arrived with the horses. At six foot two, the dark-haired rancher appeared to be a typical cowboy. But there was a lot more to Chase than met the eye. He didn't just run a horse rescue operation; he was also the heir to Parker Oil. And if you looked closely, you'd see he had on an expensive pair of boots, rather than the dusty, battered pair a ranch hand might wear.

Graham greeted his friend with a handshake, then introduced him to Jonah. The boy didn't give Chase much attention, but his dark, sour expression lightened when he spotted the first horse coming out of the trailer.

"Why is that one so skinny?" Jonah asked, pointing to a roan gelding.

"This is Barney," Chase said. "He was in an equine hospital before he came to my ranch. He's doing fairly well now, but you should have seen him two months ago."

"Was he sick?" the boy asked.

"No, he was abused and neglected. He was just skin and bones when I got him. But he was one of the lucky ones where he used to live. The other two horses were in such bad shape they had to be put down."

The boy grimaced. "That sucks. Someone should have knocked his owner's lights out. What happened to the guy?"

"He was charged with animal cruelty and neglect," Chase said.

The boy swore under his breath. "I hope he got life in prison."

"I'm afraid the penalties aren't that steep," Chase said. "But he's being punished."

"Here." Chase handed Barney's lead rope to the teen. "I'll get another horse."

"What am I supposed to do with him?" Jonah asked, but Chase was already back at the trailer.

"Give him a gentle stroke," Graham said. "Let him know that he can trust you, that you won't hurt him. Barney and the horses we're getting haven't seen much human kindness, if any. So they tend to get spooked easily. But he'll respond to a soothing voice and a soft touch."

For a moment, Graham thought the kid might balk at the suggestion. Instead he eased closer to the gelding and stroked his neck.

"You know," Jonah said, "when Brad told me you guys kept rescue horses, I figured they were wild mustangs."

"The Bureau of Land Management has strict fencing and corral rules for adoptive owners of the mustangs, but we could end up with some."

Chase returned with a chestnut mare. "This is Suzy Q."

"What happened to her?" Jonah asked. "Was she starved, too? She doesn't look as skinny as Barney."

"Suzy is a PMU mare from a farm in Canada. She was repeatedly impregnated for her urine, which was used in making drugs like Premarin, which are used to treat menopause. In her case, she was kept confined in a stall for six of the eleven months of her pregnancy. She couldn't turn around, groom herself or lie down. And her water intake was regulated to produce a maximum-estrogen urine."

"Dang," the boy said. "That's a crappy life."

"Yeah, it was pretty brutal." Chase gave the mare

a pat on the neck. "The United States has some strict laws about that these days, and Canada is starting to crack down on them. Unfortunately, the whole business is thriving in China now."

"What business?" the boy asked.

"Gathering urine from pregnant horses," Chase said. "They attach a type of catheter over a mare's urethra that's held in place by body straps that restrict her movement. Once she foals, she's only given a short time to recover, then impregnated again. When a mare is no longer able to 'produce,' most are sold for slaughter."

"How did you get her?" Jonah asked Chase.

"There was a raid on her farm in Canada, and I was able to take her and Ginger, who you'll meet in a minute."

"So you can see these horses are going to need gentle treatment and a lot of love," Graham said.

The boy, his brow furrowed, handed over Barney's halter to Graham, then strode toward the trailer, where Chase was unloading yet another gelding, that one an Appaloosa.

Jonah reached out to stroke the animal, but it threw back its head.

"Easy, boy," Jonah said. "I won't hurt you."

"He just needs a little time to get to know you better," Graham said.

When all five of the horses had been unloaded and placed in either the corral or one of the stalls in the barn, Graham thanked Chase.

"My pleasure. I'm just glad to know these horses found a good home and will get the care they need."

"Say," Graham said. "How's your wife?"

A grin stretched across Chase's face. "Lucie's great. We couldn't be happier."

"I'm glad to hear it."

Chase had married Lucie Fortune Chesterfield ten years ago in Scotland. They'd thought his parents had taken care of the paperwork to have it annulled, only to learn recently that the union was still in force. A couple of months ago, the couple struck up a romance once more and decided to stay wed.

Lucie worked for the Fortune Foundation, which had offered to sponsor Peter's Place as one of its charities. But Graham wasn't sure he wanted the funding, especially if there were strings attached. Lucie said there wouldn't be, so he was thinking it over.

Still, while he'd appreciate the additional financial support, he wasn't sure if things would get complicated, should the whole Robinson-Fortune connection prove to be true. His father might deny it, but there was reason to believe he was lying.

So what else was new?

"Well, I'd better get home," Chase said. "Lucie and I have dinner plans tonight."

The men shook hands again; then the neighboring rancher climbed behind the wheel of his truck.

"Have fun this evening," Graham said. "We'll talk soon."

Chase nodded, then started the engine and pulled away, his trailer now empty.

Graham checked his watch before turning to Jonah. "It's nearly dinnertime. You hungry?"

"Yeah, but what about the horses? Do they need hay or grain or something? Most of them are still pretty skinny."

"They already ate this morning, so we'll feed them again after dinner. I'll show you how it's done later tonight, since that'll be one of your jobs while you're here. Then, in the morning, before breakfast, you can take care of it on your own."

"So you weren't messing with me about breakfast starting at six?"

Graham chuckled. "Nope. But you won't be sorry. Roger puts out quite a spread in the morning."

"I have to," the old rancher said. "It's a long time before lunch, and you'll have to keep up your strength."

"Dang." But instead of an eye roll or a grumble, Jonah strode over to the corral and studied Suzy Q and Ginger, the two mares that were checking out their new surroundings.

Graham stole a peek at Roger, who smiled and nodded. So far, Peter's Place appeared to be working out the way they'd hoped it would.

After dinner, Graham waited for Jonah to help Sasha with the dishes. Then, as promised, he took the teenager outside and showed him how to feed the horses.

Jonah not only listened to the instructions, but also asked a few questions. Graham filled him in the best he could. Yet while the teenager seemed to be settling in at the Galloping G, Graham knew better than to believe a complete behavior and attitude change would be easy. But so far, he liked what he was seeing.

Once the evening chores were done and the barn was secured for the night, Graham walked Jonah to his cabin and watched him set the alarm clock for five-thirty in the morning.

"There's soap in the bathroom," Graham said, "as well as towels and washcloths in the linen closet. So you shouldn't need anything."

Jonah, who'd been pretty agreeable just minutes ago, shook his head and frowned. "I can't believe there isn't a TV in here. Or even Wi-Fi. I don't know what you expect me to do at night. Or how I'm s'posed to fall asleep."

"Why not try reading? It helps me." Graham crossed the small room to the bookshelf, which he'd purposely filled with a large selection of novels that a teenage boy might find appealing. "You might like *Lord of the Rings*."

"Nah, I don't want to read that. I saw the movie a jillion times. And before my mom took away the TV in my room, I played the video game. So I know that story backwards and forwards."

Graham could have insisted that books were usually ten times better than the movies, but he kept his opinion to himself. "How about one of the Harry Potter books? I'm sure you'll find something that interests you."

The boy gave a shrug, but held tight to his scowl. "I guess I'll check 'em out. Otherwise I'll die of boredom before morning."

That was all Graham could ask. Besides, it had been his plan all along to encourage the boys to read, although he wasn't sure if Jonah had figured that out.

"Just don't get so caught up in a story that you stay up too late. I guarantee that alarm clock will go off before you know it."

"I've never been a reader. Well, not since I was in middle school. That's when my old man ran off and my life went to hell."

"I'm sorry to hear that. But you're the only one who can turn things around for yourself now."

"You sound just like Mr. Taylor."

There was a reason for that. What they'd told Jonah was true. But Graham wasn't going to preach to the kid. He'd rather lead by example. "I'll see you in the morning."

"Yeah, whatever."

Jonah started toward the bookcase, and Graham left him on his own.

After closing the cabin door, Graham stepped out into the evening and headed toward his own place. As was his habit, he glanced at the big house and the window to Roger's bedroom. The light was off, indicating the rancher had gone to bed. But the porch light burned bright.

Under the yellow glow, he spotted Sasha sitting on the porch swing again. But this time, instead of leaving her alone, he changed course, crossed the yard and approached her.

"You want company?" he asked.

She slowed the swing to a stop and smiled. "Sure."

He scanned the porch, noting the chairs were about ten feet away from her.

"You can sit with me, if you want." She patted the spot next to her.

Did he want to get that cozy? For some reason, the answer was yes. So he took a seat beside her, the swing swaying and the metal hardware creaking as he did.

"What are you thinking about?" That was probably a better way of asking *who* was on her mind.

"My girls," she said.

Not Gabe? That was a relief. She might not realize it, but she and her daughters would be much better off without that guy in their lives.

"I'm trying to decide how I'm going to support them. I can get a job, of course. I have a degree in social work, so I'm sure I can find a position in Austin. But day care is expensive, especially for an infant. On top of that, it'll be hard for me to leave a newborn with someone else."

"What about child support?" he asked.

"I'm supposed to get it, but I'm not going to count on it. Gabe never was able to keep a job. And he's always refused to work for his father."

The fact that Graham had felt the same way about working for his old man at Robinson Tech didn't sit well. He hadn't expected to have anything in common with Sasha's ex.

They sat quietly awhile, lulled into a surreal sense of contentment by the slight motion of the swing they shared. Even the creaking of the chains, springs and bolts seemed to be mesmerizing.

Or was it just the presence of the lovely woman seated beside him?

He shrugged off the possibility, unwilling to ponder just what it all meant, and asked, "So, what did you think of Jonah?"

"He's angry at the world, but I suspect that has a lot to do with his father's abandonment. And the fact that he was expected to clean the house, cook the meals and babysit while his mother was at work."

"I got that idea, too. But he needs to accept the fact that his father is gone and his mom is doing the best she can."

"There might be more to it than that," Sasha said. "While he was helping me wash the dinner dishes, he mentioned that he used to be a star pitcher on his high school baseball team. He was only a sophomore at the time, and he played varsity. But he got cut from the team because he couldn't attend practice. And the reason he couldn't was that he had to look out for his younger brother and sisters. So I think his rebellion had a lot to do with resentment."

"That would have set me off," Graham said. Then again, anything Gerald Robinson had expected of him had set him off.

"I know you and Peter got into plenty of trouble when you were Jonah's age," Sasha said, "so you should be able to relate to some of the kids you'll be taking in."

"You're probably right. In fact, if Peter hadn't died, we might have ended up with probation officers, too."

"What do you mean? What kind of things were you guys doing back then?"

"Drag racing on Smoke Tree Lane, drinking and partying every weekend. The night Peter died, we'd taken the dune buggy Roger helped us build and went camping out at Vista Verde for Labor Day weekend. And we'd really tied one on." Graham rarely talked about that time in his life, but the memory flowed freely tonight, and sharing it with Sasha felt right.

"It sounds like Uncle Roger gave you guys a lot of freedom."

"Yeah, he did. My dad had told me he didn't want us leaving the Galloping G that weekend. I rarely ever listened to him and had no intention of doing it that night, so I just nodded in agreement. But my disobedience proved to be a devastating mistake."

"What happened?" she asked. "I knew there was an accident, that Peter crashed the dune buggy. But Uncle Roger never gave me any of the details."

"I didn't tell him too much about it, either," Graham said. "Just that Peter had been drinking and decided to go out for a moonlight drive."

"If you'd rather not talk about it, I understand." She reached across the seat and took his hand, a move that surprised him nearly as much as it comforted him.

"I try not to think about it, but it crops up on me sometimes." Like it did right now.

As Graham sat beside Sasha, remembering that horrible night as if it were yesterday. He held on to her as if she could keep him from falling back into that mire of guilt he'd trudged through for nearly a year after the accident.

"We made a number of bad decisions that day. The excessive drinking, the idea Peter had to drive in the dark, the fact that he didn't take time to buckle his seat belt... I wish I could go back in time and make better choices for both of us, but I can't."

"Drinking and driving that dune buggy without wearing a seat belt was Peter's fault, not yours."

She was right. And Roger had told Graham the same thing. But accidents happened in the blink of an eye, and you could never rewind the clock, even if you would have laid down your own life to have the opportunity to do so.

She stroked her thumb across the top of his hand, warming his skin and setting his senses reeling. Had she caressed his wrist instead, she would have felt his pulse pounding.

"I hope you don't blame yourself for his death," she said.

"I did for quite a while, but not anymore."

"I'm glad to hear that. Besides, my uncle said you were with him at the end. It comforted him to know that Peter hadn't died alone."

That was true, but sitting with Peter, holding him in his arms, trying desperately to stop the blood flow until he bled out... It had been the least Graham could do, but it hadn't been enough. And no matter what alternative scenarios had played through his mind over the years, nothing could change the reality of what had happened that night.

"Peter wanted me to ride with him, but I wasn't feeling too well. I'd had a lot to drink. But as soon as I heard the crash, which happened close to our campsite, I sobered up quickly and ran to him. He'd been thrown from the dune buggy and had hit his head on something. I used my cell phone to call nine-one-one, but the reception was bad up there. Somehow I managed to tell them where we were, but we were too far away for paramedics to get to us in time."

"Was Peter in pain?" she asked. "Did he suffer?"

"Fortunately, he was unconscious and didn't feel anything, as far as I know. Knowing that and the fact that I was with him at the end gave Roger a little comfort."

Roger, who'd been in his midsixties and a widower at the time, had been devastated when he lost his only child. And Graham had been crushed to lose his best friend, especially knowing the accident could have been avoided.

Sasha continued to run her thumb over his skin, singeing him until his thoughts shifted away from that awful night and back on the here and now.

"I was in California when I got word of the accident," she said. "I wanted to be here with you and Uncle Roger, but my grandfather wouldn't let me."

He gave her hand a squeeze. "It's probably just as well that you weren't. It was a difficult time. But Roger and I leaned on each other, which helped."

Sadly, he hadn't gotten any sympathy from his own father. Instead, he'd gotten the blame for it all, as well as scolding and patronizing sermons. *You brought this all on yourself,* his old man had said. *I hope you'll finally straighten up and become more responsible.*

Graham had straightened up his act, but he'd done it as a tribute to Peter and to Roger, not as a result of anything Gerald Robinson had said.

Over the next couple of years, he and Roger had grown especially close. In fact, Graham had been far more comfortable on the Galloping G than he'd been at home. And that was as true today as it had been years ago.

"It's nice that Roger has you," Sasha said. "I'd hate to think of him living all alone."

"I don't plan to live here forever, but I'm here now."

"Are you eventually going to work for your dad's company?"

"No. That life isn't for me."

At that point, the conversation stalled, leaving him to wrestle with his thoughts, with his disappointment in his father.

Moments later, he stole a glance at Sasha, saw her brow furrowed. He supposed they were both lost in their thoughts. In fact, so much so that they were still holding hands. He really ought to pull away, but he'd be damned if he knew why he didn't.

"The moon is pretty this evening." Sasha craned her neck to get a better glimpse of it. "That's one reason I like to sit out here. The scent of night-blooming jasmine is another."

"When you were a kid, you used to sit on the porch a lot."

She turned to him, her knee pressing into his, warming him to the bone, stirring his senses yet again. "Sometimes I'd see you watching me, but you never said anything."

"I was afraid you'd tell me all your boy troubles."

She smiled and slowly shook her head. "No, I would have kept those to myself."

For a moment he was tempted to tug on her hand, to get her to look him in the eye again, to… What? Kiss her? Now, that would be a dumb move to make. As far as Graham knew, she was still pining over her husband. Besides, Sasha and her children came as a package deal.

In spite of his efforts to talk himself out of the romantic thoughts that continued to bombard him, he wasn't having much luck. The lovers' moon overhead and the scent of jasmine wouldn't let him.

But instead of kissing her, which, admittedly, he was sorely tempted to do, he gave her hand that tug. And when she gazed at him, he used his free hand to cup her cheek. "Just for the record, Gabe was a fool."

Her lips parted, almost as if she was suddenly thinking about kissing him, too. But that was crazy. He knew better.

So he released her hand and got to his feet. "I'd better turn in. It'll be morning before we know it."

Then he stepped off the porch and headed for his cabin, wondering if he'd made the right decision by walking away.

Chapter Five

Last night, after Graham left Sasha on the porch, she'd stayed outside much longer than she would have had he not sat next to her and shared his painful memory.

She hadn't expected any of it—his company on the swing or his painful recollection of Peter's accident—but she was glad he'd opened up to her. As he did, her heart had gone out to him, and without a single thought of the consequences, she'd reached for his hand.

The moment she'd wrapped her fingers around his, she realized he might pull away from her, just as he'd always done when she tried to touch him in the past. But this time, he'd not only accepted her comfort, but also seemed to appreciate it.

As he'd held her hand, the warmth and gentle strength of his grip, as well as the intimacy of their conversation, stirred her once-tender heart back to life. And for the first time in years, Gabe Smith and his self-ish ways had been the last things on her mind.

Then, when Graham cupped her cheek and gazed into her eyes, her heart wasn't the only thing that stirred. Her old crush rose from the ashes, resurrected and as strong as ever, and her thoughts took a romantic turn.

If the baby hadn't chosen to kick her at that very moment, reminding her that she was seven months pregnant, she might have thought…

No, the very idea had been too wild to ponder. Graham had only tried to be brotherly, to do and say what her cousin would have, if Peter had been alive and seated with her on the swing. He'd just wanted to make her feel better about her divorce and to validate what she already knew—that Gabe wasn't worth the grief.

Graham had been right about that, too. It was a conclusion Sasha had come to years before their split. She probably should have admitted that last night, but she'd been so stunned by Graham's touch, by the intensity of his gaze, that those old girlish dreams had gotten the better of her.

After he'd left her alone, she continued to relish the memory of what they'd just shared. When she'd finally decided to head indoors for the night, she'd glanced at Graham's cabin. The lights were off, which meant he'd probably gone to sleep. But why wouldn't he have dozed off? There hadn't been any romantic thoughts and yearnings to keep him lying awake.

Her gaze had drifted to the other cabin, the new one where Jonah was staying. On the other hand, the teenager's bedroom light still blazed bright. His rebellion might have gotten him into trouble, but he was in a good place now. If anyone could reach him, it would be Graham and Roger.

The more Sasha had thought about what the two men intended to do with the Galloping G, the more she wanted to be a part of it. Considering their character and what they'd been through, Roger and Graham would undoubtedly become solid mentors those teenagers could look up to.

She shut off the porch light and entered the house, ready to call it a night. When she checked the clock in her bedroom, it was nearly ten o'clock, so she undressed and climbed into bed, exhausted. But her thoughts remained on Peter's Place. She even dreamed about it.

By the time she woke the next morning, she had a plan of her own. She would stay on the Galloping G and work with Graham and her uncle to help those boys get a new perspective in life. She certainly had the right college degree for a job like that. Besides, she'd always had a heart for kids, especially the rebellious kind like Graham and Peter used to be.

As she showered, she realized that the burden she'd been carrying when she first arrived had lifted completely, and a smile stretched across her face. She continued to think about her newly hatched plan while she dressed for the day and couldn't wait to share it with Graham and Uncle Roger.

It was amazing. The ranch had been more than just a place to gather her thoughts and make a plan for the

future. The Galloping G—or rather, Peter's Place—
was her future!

And for the first time in ages, that future looked
brighter than it ever had.

Graham's stomach rumbled in complaint, reminding him that the coffee he'd drunk and the banana he'd
eaten wasn't going to keep him going until lunchtime.
But he hadn't wanted to be around Sasha this morning, so he was trying to avoid the kitchen in the main
house, where Roger was undoubtedly fixing breakfast.

Had she realized how close he'd come to kissing her
last night? Or how he'd lain awake for hours, stretched
out in the dark, just thinking about her? He'd also pondered just what his romantic interest in her might mean.

He'd tried to shake it off and talk himself out of
whatever he was thinking and feeling, but in spite of
his best effort, it wasn't working. He'd just have to avoid
her until he had it all sorted out and knew how to deal
with it.

As he made his way through the barn, he checked
the paddocks where Barney and King, the other gelding, were stabled. From the looks of things, Jonah had
listened last night and done as he'd been instructed.
Even the bucket of oats was sealed properly.

Graham had just stepped out of the barn and into the
yard when his cell phone rang. He glanced at the screen,
recognized his older brother's name and answered.

Ben Fortune Robinson was the chief operating officer at Robinson Tech, a job well suited to the competent

businessman who dressed impeccably and took a commanding lead in the family, as well as the corporation.

After greeting each other, they made the usual small talk.

"How's Peter's Place coming along?" Ben asked.

Graham told him about Jonah moving in, although he didn't go into detail about the boy's past or his struggles. "He's only been here a couple of days, but he seems to be settling in nicely. And he's good with the rescue horses."

"How many do you have?" his brother asked.

"Chase delivered the first five yesterday. I hope to have more by the end of the month."

"I'm glad to hear that."

Something told Graham his brother hadn't called to chat. It wasn't his style. "So, what's up, Ben?"

"Well, for one thing, Zoe asked me to set up another family meeting."

Ever since learning that their father might have once been known as Jerome Fortune, a black sheep in that wealthy family, the siblings had been struggling with the news. First of all, Jerome was reportedly dead. Or was he?

Ben had been pursuing leads and clues for months and was determined to prove that their father's real name wasn't actually Gerald Robinson, that he'd been born Jerome Fortune. Graham had to admit it seemed possible, considering all he knew about his father. In fact, Ben was so convinced that he'd taken on the Fortune name, something Graham would be reluctant to do, even if it did pan out.

To further complicate the Robinson family dynamics, several of their illegitimate half siblings had turned up over the past few months. As if a family of eight wasn't big enough.

Graham had been disappointed in his father's romantic antics ever since he'd been a kid and found him embracing their nanny in the dressing room near the pool. And in some ways, Graham was still as rebellious when it came to his old man as Jonah was with his.

Yet as much as he'd like to tell Ben they could all meet without him, that he didn't give a squat who Gerald might or might not have been, he couldn't bring himself to do it.

"When and where?" Graham asked.

"My place. It's not easy setting up something that works with everyone's schedule. But I'm shooting for a week from next Saturday, at two o'clock. Is that okay with you?"

They might have a few more boys by then, but they had hired a teacher now. And they were interviewing a couple of counselors to be on staff. So he wouldn't be leaving Roger in a pinch. "Sure, Ben, that's fine. I'll be there."

"Great. And, by the way, I have some news. *Good* news."

"What's that?"

"Ella and I are expecting a baby."

An unexpected emotion slammed into Graham, making it difficult to speak. His brother was having a baby with the woman he loved?

He was happy for Ben, of course. But at the same time, a niggle of jealousy wormed its way through his chest.

How could that be? Graham had rarely envied anyone, yet for some crazy reason, he suddenly felt as though he'd like to trade places with Ben.

"Congratulations," he managed to say. "That *is* good news."

And it was. So why the jealousy?

The back door squeaked open, and Sasha walked out onto the stoop, her hand resting on her baby bump. It was then that reality struck, taunting him with the truth.

Why couldn't it be Graham's child she was carrying?

Damn. Where had that thought come from? Graham wasn't the kind of guy who'd dreamed of being a husband and father. He sure as hell hadn't looked up to his old man. And the marriage between his parents had been strained more often than not. There hadn't actually been any outward hostility between them, but their marriage wasn't what he'd call warm or loving.

As far as Graham could figure, his mom put up with a lot from his dad—like the long absences and the shortness of affection—because she liked the perks, both financial and social, of being married to Gerald Robinson. And she hadn't wanted to do anything to rock the boat.

Still, his mother might have been good at faking a happy marriage in public, but not at home. Even as a child, Graham was pretty observant. And it seemed to him that the cooler his mother became toward his father, the more his dad withdrew and stayed away. And the more Gerald was gone from home, the chillier things got between the couple.

"Well, I'd better let you get back to work," Ben said. "I'd hate to read in the paper that one of those teenagers burned down the Galloping G while you were talking on the phone."

Graham smiled. "I won't be taking in any pyromaniacs—as far as I know. But I'd better get back to work."

"I'll see you next Saturday," Ben said, before ending the call.

Even after slipping his cell phone back into his pocket, Graham couldn't help pondering his brother's news. Ella was having Ben's baby. They'd be watching her womb grow big with child, knowing they'd created a son or daughter together.

Again, Graham glanced at the stoop. Sasha wasn't there anymore. A quick scan of the yard told him she'd gone out to the corral, where Jonah was helping Maddie offer Suzy Q an apple chunk.

The boy smiled at something the pretty mother said, and Graham wished he could overhear their conversation.

Hell, even though he had every right to join them, he turned around and headed for the barn.

There was something very wrong about having such intense feelings for someone he used to think of as a kid sister. Not to mention which, Sasha was still legally married and pregnant with another man's child. He'd have to keep his inappropriate emotions—and his sexual desire for her—under wraps. And right now the best way to do that was to steer clear of her.

But damn, he was hungry.

And not just for breakfast.

* * *

Sasha followed the sounds and aroma of brewing coffee and sizzling sausage to the kitchen, where Uncle Roger was busy fixing breakfast. A yellow mixing bowl sat on the counter, next to the old waffle iron that was plugged into an outlet and heating up. Roger glanced at the stove and into the cast-iron skillet, where the links of spicy meat were frying.

Maddie, her hair still sleep-tousled and in need of a mother's touch, was dressed for the day and wearing her boots. She stood on a chair she'd pulled up next to Roger so she could watch him work. At the round, old-style oak table, Jonah sat patiently waiting to eat, a large glass of orange juice in front of him.

"Where's Graham?" Sasha asked. She assumed he was still outside doing chores and that he would come inside shortly.

"He was here a while ago." Uncle Roger stepped to the right and lowered the flame under the links of sausage. "He poured coffee into a disposable foam cup, grabbed a banana from the fruit bowl and then went out again. He said he wasn't hungry."

That was odd. Breakfast was the biggest meal of the day. And hadn't Graham said he always looked forward to eating in the ranch house with Roger?

He wasn't avoiding her, was he?

Had he felt uneasy last night after telling her Gabe was a fool? Had he thought she'd been gaping at him like a lovesick puppy?

She probably had been, but she hadn't meant to. It

was just that the kindness in his eyes and his gentle touch had stirred something deep within her.

But Graham wasn't the only who felt uneasy or foolish. Sasha felt that way, too, because she still yearned for a man who'd never been interested in her before and surely wasn't now. How could he be when he was single and unencumbered, and she would soon be the divorced mother of two?

Graham had only meant to be kind and supportive. And after she'd connected nonexistent dots, she'd imagined that he might want to kiss her.

Gathering her dignity, she shook off the silly musing and studied her daughter, who was her top priority these days. Maddie had once loved party shoes and dresses as a preschooler, but she now favored jeans and cowgirl apparel. She loved being on the Galloping G and had already had her first riding lesson, and if Graham and Uncle Roger weren't so busy, she'd have another scheduled soon. So, if Sasha intended to stay here for the time being, she wasn't doing anyone any good by allowing herself to ponder fruitless dreams.

Rather than continue standing frozen in the doorway, wondering why Graham wasn't here, she crossed the kitchen, removed a teapot from the cupboard and filled it with water. Then, after placing it on one of the empty burners on the stove, she went to the pantry and removed a box of herbal teabags.

"What's for breakfast?" she asked, although she could see for herself what Roger was preparing.

Maddie, who still stood atop that chair, turned to Sasha and flashed a gap-toothed smile. "Waffles with bananas!" She reached for the can of whipped cream. "And I get to spray this on top!"

"Sounds yummy." Sasha glanced at the teenager, who'd just finished chugging down the entire glass of OJ. "Good morning, Jonah. Did you sleep well?"

The boy shrugged. "I guess so. But I'm not used to it being so quiet outside. Our apartment is on a busy street in Austin, and it's next to a rowdy bar. Plus, I used to sleep with the TV on."

Sasha's first thought was one of sympathy for the kid, but then she remembered Jonah's mother and how hard she was working to provide a home for her fatherless children—something Sasha could relate to.

She wondered if Graham had given any thought to the parents of the rebellious kids he hoped to help. The ones who had moms like Jonah's might need someone to talk to, someone who could help bridge the gap between parent and child. Someone like Sasha, who was also a single parent trying to raise her daughters on her own.

It was going to take that proverbial village to help the boys who came to live at Peter's Place and their families. And Sasha was eager to do her share.

She'd meant to talk to Graham about it after breakfast, when Jonah wasn't within earshot, but that plan wasn't going to work. So she might as well talk to Graham now, if she could find him. And since she had something important to say, she would just act as though nothing had happened last night.

Actually, nothing had.

"I'll be back," she announced to the kitchen crew.

Then she walked out the backdoor and went in search of Graham.

She found him at the side of the barn, loading up the Gator with wooden posts and tools. There was a determination in him today, an intensity she hadn't noticed before. His very movements and the crease in his brow only made him more attractive, more appealing.

Great. As if his sturdy, muscular build and gorgeous face weren't enough. But she pressed on.

Upon her approach, she said, "Good morning."

He glanced up, wearing only the hint of a smile, and gave a little nod. "Mornin'." Then he continued to stack fence posts into the back of the Gator, his biceps flexing and his black T-shirt stretching with the effort.

Ignoring the awkwardness that settled over her, she continued. "I'd like to talk to you."

He stopped what he was doing, yet his expression was one of apprehension.

Oh, good grief. He didn't fear that she'd ask him to go on a date or something, did he?

"Talk to me about what?" he asked.

"A couple ideas I had for Peter's Place."

At that, his masculine features softened and he gave her his full attention.

Again she wondered if she'd been right, if he'd been avoiding her because he'd sensed her attraction to him. But she cast the possibility aside and told him her idea about moving in with Uncle Roger and using her education to help out in some way.

"You mean," he said, tilting his head slightly to the side, "you want to be a counselor?"

"Yes. Or whatever else you might want me to do. I thought I might even develop a counseling program for the boys' parents."

He lifted his hat and raked his fingers through his short, light brown hair.

Was her question that difficult for him to answer? You'd think he'd... Well, he might not jump at the chance to have her help, but surely he wasn't opposed to it. Then again, maybe he wanted only male counselors for some reason.

She'd argue that the boys would need to learn how to relate to women, too.

Finally, he said, "That's a good idea. The families and parents will need to make a few adjustments, especially if the boys are going to ever return home. And Roger mentioned that you had a degree in social work."

"I've yet to use it," she admitted, "but I was an A student. At one time, I'd planned to get a job with the state or county. But you know how the old saying goes, 'Bloom where you're planted.' And it appears that I've been planted here." She tossed him a breezy smile, hoping he'd see the wisdom in her words, the truth of it, as well as the possibilities.

A slow grin tugged at his lips. "Yeah, I guess that's true. I know Roger would be thrilled to have you join the team."

"But what about you?" she asked. "I don't want to upset your plans."

He lifted a single shoulder and gave a halfhearted shrug. "Actually, it might be easier working with someone we know rather than a stranger."

Before she could rejoice in her victory, the screen door at the back of the house opened and slammed shut. They both turned to the sound and spotted Maddie making her way across the yard. She wore her cowboy hat now, covering the tangles Sasha had yet to help her comb out, and had something in her hand.

"Mr. Graham?" the child called out, drawing the adults' attention and diffusing the situation.

"Yes," he answered. "I'm over here, honey. By the Gator."

Whatever she held had been wrapped in a napkin, and she handed it to Graham. "Uncle Roger said to give this to you 'cause you're probably hungry."

"What is it?" he asked.

"A piece of waffle with butter and a smidge of syrup. I wanted to spray out a lot of whip cream on it, but Uncle Roger wouldn't let me. He said it would be too messy and sticky to carry."

"He was right about that." Graham took it from her and thanked her, but he didn't unwrap the napkin.

"Jonah told me he gets to work with the rescue horses," Maddie said. "He said you just pet them and talk soft and give them treats. Can I do that, too?"

Graham looked to Sasha for an answer. Either he didn't mind and wanted her opinion or he didn't want to hurt the little girl's feelings.

"I think it's best if you have a few more riding lessons with one of the other horses first," Sasha said.

Rather than accept Sasha's answer, Maddie turned to the handsome cowboy, her eyes squinting in the morning sun. "I can't wait to go riding again, but can I at least give Suzy and Ginger pieces of apple? Jonah said it's easy. You just hold your hand open, like this, so your fingers don't get in the way and get chomped on." She stretched out her palm to show the man.

Graham smiled. "Yep, that's how it's done. I'm sure the horses would like that."

"Good! And can I come to work with you on the fence, too—like Jonah gets to do today? I'm very strong." To prove her point, she flexed her biceps.

Graham reached out and gripped her little arm with his thumb and index finger as if gauging her strength. He released her and let out a slow whistle. "Well, what do you know, Maddie? You're pretty darn strong. But I don't think you're ready to tackle the fence yet."

"Then can I watch? I'll be good. And quiet."

Graham again glanced at Sasha. "That's up to your mom."

Surely he was just being kind and didn't want to disappoint her daughter by saying no.

"I'd rather you stayed near the house today," Sasha said. "I have some cooking to do and will need your help."

Maddie frowned, clearly preferring ranch work over the kitchen detail.

"I'll tell you what," Graham said. "I'll come up with some cowboy chores for you to do when your mom doesn't need you in the house."

"Okay. I can do that." The child brightened. "You can count on me, pardner."

Graham smiled. Apparently, he'd known that she'd prefer to do ranch chores. And the fact that he'd acted on that caused Sasha's heart to melt like a chocolate Kiss in the noonday sun. Maddie was clearly enamored with the man.

So was Sasha, for that matter.

But it wasn't about *her* feelings. It was about Maddie's. Graham seemed to like the little girl and didn't appear to be dismayed by either her presence or her offer to help. At least, not yet. But would he come to resent her, as Gabe had?

"Maddie," Sasha suggested, "would you go inside and tell Uncle Roger I'm about ready for that waffle now? And I'd love to have bananas and a little whipped cream on mine."

"Okay," Maddie said. "I'll fix the top just the way you like it." Then she turned away and hurried back to the house, providing Sasha with an opportunity to speak to Graham about the child's apparent hero worship.

When the screen door slammed shut, Sasha said, "I know you have plenty of work to do—and not just today. So I hope she doesn't become a pest."

"Like you used to be?" he asked, a grin slapped on his face.

"Yes, but you were stuck with me."

His gaze locked on hers, turning her heart inside out and shaking up everything she treasured. Those old childish feelings she'd tried so hard to tamp down rushed back front and center, only they were all grown up this time around.

But that wouldn't do. It wouldn't do at all.

She crossed her arms, hoping to put a lid on all she

held inside. "If you had been rude or taken a swat at me, my uncle would have had your hide."

He winked. "That's true."

"But don't worry. I'll find plenty of things to keep Maddie busy, chores and activities she can do in the house."

"She's a cute kid, and I actually enjoy talking to her. I never know what she's going to say next. But I'll tell you what. If she ever becomes a bother, I'll let you know."

"I'd appreciate that."

He studied her for a moment, and then his brow furrowed. "Are you really concerned about her becoming a nuisance?"

"Actually, I'm more concerned about her bothering *you*."

"Don't worry about me. I have seven brothers and sisters, remember?"

He didn't talk about them very much, so sometimes it was easy to forget that he hadn't been an only child.

"Yes, I know," Sasha said. "It's just that Maddie's father had very little patience with her."

"That surprises me. She's a sweet kid."

"It surprised me, too." Sasha could have gone on to list all of Gabe's shortcomings, but she didn't. After all, what would that say about her and her ability to choose a solid, dependable and loving mate?

"Did Gabe's impatience have anything to do with the reason you two split up?" Graham asked.

"That was part of it, I guess." Again, she hated to

reveal all the heartbreaking details, but she decided to share one. "Just for the record, it was Gabe who left."

"I'm sorry."

"Don't be. It was probably for the best."

When Graham didn't object or quiz her further, she added, "I'll be the first to admit that our life together was far from perfect, but I made a commitment to stick it out for the long haul."

"And he didn't."

"That's about the size of it." If Gabe had meant those vows, he wouldn't have found it so easy to leave her when she learned she was pregnant a second time.

"Anyway," she said, "enough of that. And back to Maddie. She's never felt especially close to her father, so I think that's one reason she's eager to strike up a relationship with Uncle Roger and with you. But I don't want her to get too clingy, so let me know if she does."

Graham cupped her jaw again. As his calloused thumb made circular strokes on her cheek, every nerve ending in her body sparked to life, and a bolt of heat zigzagged to her very core.

"Don't worry," he said. "Your daughter's a sweet-heart. I can handle her."

Maybe so. Graham appeared to be a kindhearted and amazing man with the patience of Job when it came to kids and teenagers.

But what about Sasha herself? Could she handle being around Graham without revealing the feelings she still harbored for him, feelings she could no longer attribute to a childish crush?

She'd have to. Graham Robinson could have any

woman he set his sights on. And there was no way he'd ever choose a pregnant woman whose baby bump made her feel as big as Uncle Roger's barn—and just as sexy. And while her physical condition alone would surely hamper any chance of romance between them, that didn't bother her nearly as badly as the truth.

Graham had never considered her a viable love interest and probably never would.

Chapter Six

On Saturday evening, Brad Taylor called Graham's cell. This time he had the number and the name straight. "Hey, Graham. How's Jonah doing?"

"Actually, he's settling in better than I expected him to do at this point. He seems to enjoy working with the horses. He also has a good appetite. His only real complaint is the fact that he doesn't have a television or Wi-Fi in his cabin."

"So he's going through video-game withdrawal, huh?" Taylor chuckled.

"Yep, but he'll survive and be a better kid for it. In fact, I checked in on him a few minutes ago, and he was reading *Lord of the Flies*."

"Good. It sounds like Peter's Place was a smart move

for him." Taylor paused a beat, then cleared his throat. "Are you and Roger ready to take in another boy?"

Adding another teenager to the mix was sure to change the dynamics, but that wasn't necessarily a bad thing. "Sure. We'll take him."

"His name is Ryan Maxwell. He's sixteen and was caught vandalizing heavy equipment at a construction site near his home."

"What was his excuse? Boredom?"

"Yeah, pretty much. But I think it runs deeper than that. It usually does. From what I can see from his school records, he was in gifted and honors classes up until two years ago, about the time his parents were killed in a car accident."

"So you think he's rebelling because of his grief?"

"Yeah, maybe a little. But he's angry, too. His maternal uncle was granted custody of him, and that guy is a real tool. He hasn't been able to hold down a job and would rather go out drinking each night than stay home with the kid. This is Ryan's first brush with the law, and I'd like it to be the last."

"We'll see what we can do about that."

"I'll email you a full report on him this evening," Taylor said. "Then I'll bring him out to the ranch on Monday, around three o'clock."

The call had no more than ended when a knock sounded on Graham's cabin door. He assumed it might be Jonah, but when he answered, he found Sasha on his porch. She held a foil-covered plate in her hand.

"Hi," he said.

"I wasn't sure what you planned to eat tonight, but

Roger made carne asada tacos, rice and beans. There was plenty left over, so I brought you some."

Apparently, she had no idea he'd been trying his best to steer clear of her, even if it meant eating canned soup and a ham sandwich for dinner.

He took the plate and thanked her. "Actually, I already ate, but I have a little room left for a taco."

She blessed him with a pretty smile that turned him every which way but loose and made him wonder if avoiding her hadn't been such a good idea after all.

"Have you given any thought to letting me work with the boys or their parents?" she asked.

To be honest, he hadn't had a chance to run it by Roger, who'd undoubtedly love the idea. And while working closely with Sasha wasn't going to be easy for Graham, he couldn't very well tell her no.

"I'm okay with it, if you are. How soon do you want to start?"

"Actually, I've been trying to work with Jonah already. I think he likes me. At least, he's opened up some."

"Good, I'm glad to hear that. I'm sure you'll stay busy. Brad Taylor, Jonah's probation officer, is bringing a second boy Monday afternoon."

She brightened. "That's good. I'm sure Jonah will be glad to have another kid his age staying here."

"I'm sure he will."

"The Galloping G is a great place for a boy to become a man," she added.

It had certainly helped Graham to grow up and turn his life around. But as much as he wanted to see Peter's

Place come together, his business expertise could be best used to apply for state grants and to secure more donations for their nonprofit organization. So he didn't plan to remain working here forever.

"Just so you know," he said, "I'm behind Peter's Place a hundred percent. But I won't always be living in one of the cabins."

"Are you going to build a bigger house?" she asked. "I'm sure you'd be more comfortable."

She didn't get it.

"Once the foundation is up and running, I'm going to move to Austin," he explained. "But I won't just oversee it from afar. I'll visit regularly."

Her eyes widened, and her lips parted. "What do you plan to do in the city?"

"I grew up in a technologically astute household, so I have a certain savvy about that stuff, too. I also have an MBA. So while I enjoy working on the ranch, I won't be doing this the rest of my life."

"Are you going to start your own company?" She wrinkled her brow, then shook her head. "I'm sorry. I didn't mean to make that sound as if I didn't think you had any business sense. I just thought you loved…"

Her comment trailed off, but he knew what she'd been about to say. "I enjoy working the land, riding horses and spending time with Roger. But that doesn't mean I plan to play cowboy until I'm stooped and bent."

"I…" She paused and bit down on her bottom lip. "That's not what I meant."

No, but it was what she'd implied. Time and again, his father had accused him of all that and more.

"I'm not leaving tomorrow," Graham said.

She seemed to chew on that awhile, then began to nod. "Of course. But what plans do you have for financing Peter's Place? Before I tell Uncle Roger that I plan to stay here and help, I want to know the boys' home is secure."

"Don't worry about money. I'll make sure the ranch is solvent. And as a side note, the Fortune Foundation has offered to make it one of its charities. That hasn't been officially decided, but either way, there shouldn't be any financial concerns."

The wrinkle in her brow deepened, and her mind appeared to be going into overtime.

Something must be bothering her. But what?

Graham's announcement slammed into Sasha like a bull out of the shoot, although she shouldn't be surprised to hear that he planned to move on. After all, he was a Robinson, which meant he had a slew of options available to him, especially in the city. And while she hadn't expected him to stay on the Galloping G forever, he'd become as much a part of the ranch as her uncle was.

Was that a new decision? Was he leaving because she'd decided to stay? Did she make him that uncomfortable?

Graham studied her intently, as if he knew just how she felt about his pending departure.

"What's the matter?" he asked.

She couldn't very well admit that she'd been having romantic feelings for him, that she'd hoped... She slowly shook her head. "Nothing's wrong."

She was a big girl. She'd get over the loss. But what about Maddie? The little girl had so much love to give. And while Maddie had never been very close to her father, Sasha still worried about the effect Gabe's abandonment might have on her when it came to her future relationships with boys and men.

Even at seven, Maddie appeared to be looking for a male influence in her life. And once she'd met Graham, she seemed to have set her sights on him. Sasha didn't mind, since he was one of the white hats. Maybe that hadn't always been the case, but he certainly was nowadays. Yet Maddie's adoration was still a concern. The child seemed to be dead set on making friends with Graham, working with him on the ranch and getting more of those promised riding lessons. It was all she ever talked about.

In fact, if Sasha hadn't caught her running out the door on several occasions and redirected her, Maddie would be following her cowboy hero around from sunup until sundown.

So how would she feel when Graham moved on to greener pastures, something her father had done?

"I can tell something's bothering you, Sassy." Graham eased closer, so much so that Sasha caught a whiff of his musky scent.

She would never admit it, but she couldn't help feeling that her cowboy hero was about to abandon her, too.

But at least, for the time being, Graham wasn't going anywhere. Instead he moved closer still. "Are you concerned about me leaving you and your uncle on the ranch to deal with the boys on your own? If so, don't be. I've already sorted through potential job applicants and will line up competent people to work with you, experienced professionals who can guide you. And like I said, I'll return regularly—and often."

"No, it's not that. It's just…" No way could Sasha open up and reveal all the emotion she had bottled up inside. Instead she would only share a part of it. "I'm worried about Maddie. She seems to have really latched on to you. And I don't want her to wind up disappointed when you leave."

"I can understand that. She's a great kid, and I wouldn't want to see her hurt, either."

Tears welled in Sasha's eyes and she swiped them away. "I'm sorry. It's just that her father pretty much turned his back on her."

Gabe had walked out on Sasha, as well, but she really hadn't been bothered by his leaving. In a lot of ways, it had been a relief.

"Don't worry," Graham said. "I'll be considerate of Maddie's feelings and won't walk away without a backward glance." He placed his hand on her shoulder, and the heat of his touch spiraled deep inside her. The intensity in his gaze and the promise he made filled her with…warmth. And something more. They'd barely broached a friendship as adults, yet she hoped that they'd…that he'd…

Oh for Pete's sake. She didn't dare voice it, even to herself.

As they continued to study each other, she hoped her jumbled thoughts and emotions weren't evident in her expression.

"I'm not like Gabe," Graham said.

"Yes, I know." That was part of why Sasha was so drawn to him now.

Of course, she'd always thought the world of Graham. Sometimes late at night, while Gabe had been away on a business trip or at the office or at some meeting she'd suspected wasn't related to his work at all, Sasha had felt lonely and neglected. And when those blue evenings came, she would find herself thinking of the handsome teenage Graham and imagining him all grown up.

She knew that she'd been idealizing him at the time. She'd done the same thing with Gabe when they first started dating.

And while she'd come to the conclusion that marrying Gabe had been a mistake, she wouldn't regret it. Otherwise, she wouldn't have Maddie—or the baby she'd yet to meet.

"Don't get me wrong," Sasha said as she placed her hand on her baby bump and felt her little one shift position. "I cared for Gabe, but I found it difficult to respect him."

She hadn't planned to explain, but maybe it was best if he understood there were many reasons her marriage had failed.

"For one thing," she admitted, "Gabe was so determined to make it on his own and without the help of his dad that he refused to work for the family company."

"I'd be the last one to criticize a man for not wanting to work with his father," Graham said.

The fact that the two men had that one similarity crossed her mind. But that was different. Wasn't it?

She shook off the comparison. "I'm not saying he should have worked for his father. I understood why he wanted to do something on his own, which was understandable. But that wasn't the problem. Gabe couldn't seem to keep a job. Each time something didn't go his way, he'd quit. Believe it or not, during the eight years we were married, he probably had ten different employers."

"I can see why you'd be disappointed in him. Sometimes a man has to swallow his pride and learn to get along with others." Gabe reached out and stroked her shoulder and upper arm, offering her compassion and...

There she went again, imagining all sorts of motives behind the glimmer in his amazing blue eyes.

"Like I told you before," Graham said, "Gabe was a fool. He didn't have any idea how good he had it."

Sasha's heart rumbled in her chest, vibrating to the point she feared it might stifle the words before they left her mouth. "You have no idea how much I appreciate you saying that."

"It's true." He placed his hand along her jaw, then brushed a kiss on her forehead in what was surely meant to be a brotherly or friendly gesture.

But in spite of her better judgment, she gazed up at him. When their eyes met, he spoke to her in a way he never had—only without words.

The sweet kiss he'd given her brow had merely triggered something deeper, something stronger. Before she could contemplate just what that might be and what it might mean, he lowered his mouth to hers.

The moment their lips met, friendship and brotherly love flew by the wayside. And *ka-pow*! Her head swirled and the earth shook. But she'd barely tasted him and lifted her arms to slip them around his neck when he pulled away.

"I'm sorry," he said. "That was completely out of line. I have no idea why I did that. But it won't happen again."

Did he fear them getting any closer? Had he momentarily forgotten how complicated a romantic relationship with her would be? She certainly had. But reality struck hard.

"Listen," he said, nodding toward the Gator, "I've enjoyed talking to you, but I need to get back to work."

Then he did just that, leaving her alone in the middle of the yard, stunned by the strength of her desire and amazed at the feelings his brief kiss had evoked. Yet as he walked way, dashing the hope she'd dared to grasp, her heart cramped.

He'd called her ex a fool, but Sasha was the real fool. Graham could have any woman he wanted, especially when he moved to Austin. Why would he settle for a soon-to-be mother of two?

Either way, whatever special moment they'd shared was now over. And while her head told her why that was for the best, her heart refused to hear it and tears welled in her eyes.

She wasn't sure what she'd actually felt for Graham when she was younger, a crush or something much stronger than that. But she was grown up now and definitely falling head over heart in love.

Yet what good would that do her when she felt as big as a Brahma bull?

In any event, there was no way Graham had any interest in dating her. And even if he did, what man in his right mind would want to take on the fatherhood of a seven-year-old *and* a newborn in one fell swoop?

Graham was the epitome of a handsome and eligible bachelor. He was in his thirties, so he'd undoubtedly had plenty of admirers over the years.

No, if he was actually interested in having a family, he'd have one already.

The truth of that realization stole what little hope she'd harbored. Before returning to the house, she swiped the tears from her eyes and did her best to shake off the ache in her heart.

Her love for Graham would continue to be her secret for the rest of her life.

After walking away from Sasha, Graham thought about that kiss and swore under his breath. It might have lasted only a moment, but the effects had knocked him completely off stride. And in spite of his best intentions, he wasn't been able to keep his mind on anything else for the next couple of days.

He'd slipped up and let his hormones rule his brain. Damn. He still couldn't believe he'd actually let a brotherly kiss morph into something much more.

Thank God he'd finally come to his senses. He'd also made himself scarce, staying busy and away from the house and yard, something that should have been easy to do on a working ranch. Instead keeping his distance from Sasha—and even Maddie!—had been as tough as cutting into a serving of rawhide with a butter knife.

Even at night, after he locked himself away in his cabin, he still couldn't escape. He kept reliving that precious moment over and over. The kiss might have been brief, but it lasted long enough for him to know how good it had been, how good they could be together. And now that Graham realized the kind of passion he and Sasha could stir up, he feared that one kiss wasn't going to be enough to quench his thirst for her.

What had he been thinking?

That was the problem. He *hadn't* been thinking. At least, not clearly.

Even now, days later, it didn't seem to matter that Sasha was pregnant with another man's baby and that she had a seven-year-old in need of a father. For some reason, her motherhood seemed to only add to her appeal. So that was why Graham had chosen to stay away, to begin eating alone in his cabin. Maybe, if he were a better cook, he wouldn't mind.

But who was he kidding? It wasn't the meals he was missing.

Fortunately, he had a damn good reason to leave the ranch this afternoon. It was time for that family meeting at Ben's house. Only trouble was, he was pushing the speed limit so he wouldn't be late.

Early this morning, he'd taken Jonah out to finish working on the last stretch of broken fence, and the kid had gotten cut on a piece of buried barbed wire.

He was going to be fine, but taking him to the doctor and having his wound treated had eaten a big chunk of time out of the day.

But Graham was in Austin now. And right on schedule.

Once he reached the busy street on which Ben lived, he left his truck in a downtown parking structure, then walked a block to his older brother's place.

The four-story building Ben called home was flanked by skyscrapers and a small family-run deli that had been there for years. Graham still found it hard to believe that his oldest brother would prefer living here rather than a penthouse suite.

Maybe he'd consider moving now that he was married with a baby on the way.

When Graham arrived at Ben's and stood before the dark gray door, he glanced at his wristwatch, then rang the bell. As expected, Ben's housekeeper answered.

"You're late," the stern, gray-haired woman said. "Everyone else has already arrived."

Actually, Graham was right on time, give or take a minute or two. He could have given Mrs. Stone any number of excuses, if he were so inclined—the gash on Jonah's leg, the visit to Urgent Care, the traffic he'd fought, thanks to an accident on the interstate.

Instead he clamped his mouth shut and let the housekeeper lead him to the elevator, which he rode up to the floor where Ben's old-fashioned study was located.

Someone had brought in extra chairs, all but two of them taken. His sisters Sophia and Olivia had already arrived, and so had Rachel, who'd come from

Horseback Hollow. The girls, who'd been talking quietly among themselves, looked up when Graham entered.

Ben was seated behind his desk, while Wes, his twin, had chosen a chair by the door. The two men looked similar in build and had both dark hair and blue eyes, but they were different in style and temperament.

Kiernan, their youngest brother, sat next to Wes. The only one not seated was Zoe. She stood at the terraced window, studying the busy city outside.

"Good," Ben said. "Now that Graham's here, we can get started."

Graham took an empty chair, but Zoe remained at the window, her glossy, straight brown hair hanging down her back.

"Zoe?" Ben asked. "Did you hear me?"

"Sorry." She turned away from the downtown view, but she didn't take a seat. Instead she placed her hands on her hips and smoothed the fabric of her stylish yellow sundress.

"Why don't you start by telling us why you wanted me to call this meeting?" Ben asked Zoe.

"All right." She bit down on her bottom lip, as if what she had to say would take a great effort, but her struggle didn't last long. "I have a confession to make. I've been holding back information."

All eyes zeroed in on her, and she blew out a weary sigh before continuing. "I know for a fact that Dad *is* Jerome Fortune."

It took a moment for that bit of news to register, but once it did, all the siblings began to chatter.

Ben, who'd always been the take-charge type, told

everyone to quiet down. When the murmurs ceased, he asked Zoe, "How do you know that?"

"I recognized the Fortune ring that Charles Fortune Chesterfield gave his fiancée, Alice. Dad has one just like it. So I confronted him, and he finally admitted it."

Graham slowly shook his head. He hadn't wanted to believe it, but he wouldn't put anything past their old man. If this had all come down the pike a few years ago, when he still had a king-size chip on his shoulder, he might have stormed out of the house in disgust and anger. Yet even though he had a handle on his feelings now, that didn't mean he liked being betrayed and having to accept the fact that his father had been living a lie.

Damn. They were all living that lie.

"I'm sorry for not telling you sooner," Zoe added, "but Dad didn't want anyone to know."

"Why would it matter?" Wes asked. "We deserved to know. He shouldn't have kept it a secret from us."

"The story is actually pretty shocking," Zoe said. "When Dad left the Fortune fold, he'd wanted to get away so badly he actually faked his own death to sever ties with his family."

Their old man had gone to those extremes to run away? There wasn't much about his father's decisions, choices and antics that surprised Graham, but that bit of news certainly had.

The siblings started talking over each other, clearly stunned by Zoe's revelation.

Again, Ben asked them to be quiet. Then he said, "Okay, now we have the answer. But that leaves us with another question. Should we tell Kate Fortune?"

The conversation lulled, although why wouldn't it? Cosmetics mogul Kate Fortune had been meeting with various Fortune relatives, looking for someone to run her company.

At ninety years old, Kate looked a decade younger and was still as sharp as ever. She also had more money than she could possibly spend, thanks to the success of the Fortune Youth Serum she'd developed.

Kate would probably outlive them all, but she was determined to find someone in the family to take Fortune Cosmetics to the next generation. She had her own offspring already working for her, but she thought her company needed new blood and fresh ideas. So she'd been interviewing various Fortune family members, looking for someone to take under her wing.

If she knew the Robinsons were actually Fortunes, as had been suspected, she might want to talk to them, too. But then again, Gerald—or Jerome, as he'd once been known—had always been a black sheep.

"I doubt any of us would be seriously considered," Wes said. "And even if she were to choose one of us, Dad would have a fit if he thought one of his kids had gone to work for 'The Enemy.'"

Wes had that right.

"Unfortunately," Zoe said, "the decision about who to tell may have already been taken out of our hands."

"What makes you say that?" Graham asked.

"Because..." She took another deep breath and slowly let it out. "I told Keaton Whitfield."

"You did *what*?" Ben's face grew stern, and an angry flush settled on his cheeks. But Graham could understand why. His older brother had gone in search of their father's illegitimate children and found Keaton, a half sibling who lived in England and who favored Ben in looks.

Ben swore under his breath, but Zoe didn't back down. "Keaton and I talked after Joaquin and I got back from our honeymoon. He told me that he'd located two other possible offspring of Gerald Robinson. And one of them also remembered an emerald ring with the letter *F* on it."

Ben slowly shook his head, obviously pissed.

"I didn't tell Keaton *everything*," Zoe said, "just that the Fortune connection was a real one."

Ben clucked his tongue. "I can't believe Keaton came to you and not to me."

Graham could understand that. Ben was the one who'd first met Keaton. But Graham was more focused on the fact that there were more Robinsons—or rather *Fortunes*—out there.

The siblings talked among themselves about what this might mean. Some were pleased by the news, while others had been merely unsettled by it. Graham was neither. He'd never quite fit into the family, anyway. At least, his issues with his father hadn't helped that. And now…? Hell, he wasn't sure who his family was anymore. Obviously, they weren't Robinsons. But Fortunes?

When Ben used the intercom to call Mrs. Stone and ask her to bring in refreshments, Graham told his brother he couldn't stay. "I need to get back to the ranch, so you'll have to excuse me."

"I'm afraid I need to go, too," Zoe said.

Graham placed his hand on his kid sister's back. "I'll walk you out."

As the two of them left Ben's study, Graham glanced at the woman who was a newlywed and no longer a child.

Zoe had always been close to their father and had refused to think that the man had any faults. It really wasn't that she was naive. She just tended to see the good in people.

And now Zoe, like the rest of the Robinson-Fortune brood, was beginning to see just how flawed their father was.

Graham suspected that learning the truth must have been tough on her and that admitting she'd been wrong about him, when she'd been his biggest champion, had to be very humbling.

Once they left the house and stepped onto the sidewalk, Graham said, "It must have been tough for you to make that announcement."

"It wasn't easy. I feel pretty stupid for being the lone holdout, but once I learned the truth, I needed to speak up."

"Loyalty is a virtue, Zoe. And so is admitting when you were wrong. If I ever need someone in my corner, I hope you'll step up."

She smiled. "Thank you."

As they continued toward the parking garage, the soles of her high-heeled sandals and his boots crunched on the gritty concrete.

They'd only gone a few feet when Zoe's steps slowed,

and she turned to Graham. "I take it you've been skeptical about Dad for years."

He stopped along with her and nodded. "Remember Suzette, the au pair from France?"

"Yes, but just barely. She was very pretty, with long, dark hair and big blue eyes. She also had an intriguing accent. I thought of her as a princess. So what about her?"

"I caught Dad kissing her in the dressing room by the pool."

"How old were you?"

"Eleven or twelve."

Her brow furrowed as she thought about what he'd just revealed. "What did you say when you found them?"

"Nothing, really. Dad said I'd misread what I saw and that I'd be in big trouble if I told anyone."

"Did you?" she asked.

"Misinterpret what I saw?" Graham shook his head. "No, I wasn't stupid."

Zoe released a pent-up sigh. "When I was little, I caught him hugging our neighbor Mrs. Caldwell at one of their New Year's Eve parties. She was crying and talking about a baby."

"Whose?"

"She didn't say, but now I can only wonder."

The two exchanged a knowing look.

"I realize now that Dad lied to me about it," Zoe said. "He told me he was only comforting her because she was upset about something. He asked me not to tell anyone because Mrs. Caldwell was embarrassed that

I'd seen her crying. He also told me that he and I had a special bond."

"That's no secret," Graham said. "But what about the baby?"

"Dad told me that I'd misunderstood what I'd heard. Apparently, our father is a very misunderstood man."

"Um, yeah. You think?" Graham slowly shook his head, amazed at his father's growing number of scandals.

"Did you keep his secret?" Zoe asked.

"I tried to tell Mom—in my own way. But she didn't take the hint."

"I'm not surprised that she turned a blind eye. She had eight kids and probably wanted to hold her marriage together. It's what most mothers would do, I guess."

Graham didn't know about that, but it was what *their* mother had done over the years. In spite of the fact that she must have known about her husband's philandering, she hadn't confronted him. At least, not that Graham had been aware of.

"Anyway," he said, "I lost respect for Dad that day."

"Is that why you were so rebellious?"

A crooked grin tugged at his lips. "I was probably born with a rebel spirit. But after seeing Dad for what he really was, I decided to disappoint him, just the way he'd disappointed me."

His kid sister seemed to think about that for a moment, then she said, "If I'd caught Dad kissing another woman, if I'd suspected any of this, I might have been tempted to rebel, too."

Graham doubted it. Zoe had always been a good

girl. But then again, she was no longer the child he remembered.

"So, how's married life?" he asked.

At the question, Zoe brightened, reminding him of how sweet and fun-loving she'd always been. "It's amazing. I love Joaquin more and more each day. You really ought to consider settling down and getting married."

Should he? He hadn't given it any thought before, but now, as he pondered the idea, Sasha, Maddie and the baby came to mind. But Sasha wasn't ready for another relationship. Her marriage had ended just months ago. She needed more time, and Graham wouldn't push himself on her.

"I never thought I was cut out for married life," he told his little sis. "But your happiness is hard to hide. So maybe, if a special woman ever lands on my doorstep, I might consider it."

As they continued to their parked vehicles, Graham pondered the idea of love and marriage, of coming home each night to a wife and kids. Again Sasha came to mind.

Had he actually found that special woman already?

Chapter Seven

Sasha stood on the porch and watched as Graham talked to Brad Taylor. She wasn't sure what she'd been expecting when the probation officer arrived with the second teenager, but certainly not the kid who'd climbed out of the white sedan.

Graham had let her read the court paperwork he'd received so she'd be prepared to meet Ryan Maxwell. As a result, she'd made the usual assumption and figured he'd be a surly and destructive delinquent.

But unlike Jonah, Ryan didn't appear to be the least bit grumpy or hardened. Instead his shoulders slumped, as though he'd been beaten down by life.

He wasn't very tall for a fifteen-year-old boy, and he was much too thin. His glasses, which he continued to adjust on the bridge of his nose, were too big for his face. But his shy, frail appearance didn't erase the seriousness of the crime he'd committed. The damage he'd done to the equipment on the job site had cost the construction company nearly ten thousand dollars, and the owner wasn't taking that lightly.

Sasha wasn't sure what had been going on in the once-studious boy's mind or what had provoked him to put dirt in the fuel tanks of those tractors. But she meant to find out.

Taylor placed a hand on Ryan's thin shoulders and looked at Graham. "Where do you want him to put his things?"

"He'll bunk with Jonah." Graham turned toward the barn and called to the other teenager.

When Jonah walked out into the yard, he furrowed his brow, clearly checking out the new kid.

"This is Ryan," Graham said as he introduced the two teenagers. "Will you take him to your cabin and show him which bunk is his?"

Jonah, who'd just begun to shake his who-gives-a-rat's-ass attitude since arriving on the Galloping G, stiffened and slipped back into his tough-guy demeanor. "Yeah. Come on."

Ryan grabbed the canvas handle of his small bag and followed Jonah. They'd only taken a few steps when Graham called out to them, "As soon as Ryan puts his things away, bring him back here."

Jonah continued on his way, but he acknowledged the order with a wave of his hand and a "Got it, boss."

At that point, Sasha quit watching from a distance and made her way toward the men. When the teenagers were out of earshot, Graham turned to Mr. Taylor. "The report didn't mention it, but I take it Ryan doesn't have many friends."

"Before his parents died," Mr. Taylor said, "he was pretty active in a math and science club. So I assume he used to have friends who shared his same interests. But that changed when he moved in with his uncle and had to switch schools. He's a loner now."

"It would seem that way," Sasha said. "The report said he damaged that equipment on his own."

"I noticed that," Graham said. "Back in the day, when I was dead set on stirring up trouble, I was much braver when I had a buddy with me."

Buddies like Peter, Sasha realized.

About that time, Uncle Roger, who'd walked out of the house moments ago, stepped off the porch, crossed the yard and joined them. "That new boy is too skinny. I'll have to fatten him up."

Sasha smiled at the older man, who loved to cook. "If anyone has the culinary skill to do that, you do."

"Jonah's certainly been eating well enough to gain weight. So it sounds like you'll be fixing a lot more biscuits and gravy, as well as those homemade cinnamon rolls." Graham chuckled and placed a hand on his flat belly. "It's a good thing I've been eating on my own these days, or I'd be putting on pounds, too."

Sasha doubted that the extra calories had anything to do with Graham's decision to avoid Roger's meals, but she wouldn't stress over it.

Turning the focus of the conversation back on their newest teenage resident, she said, "From what I gathered, Ryan skipped a grade in school and was college-bound. I suspect having his dreams shattered first by the death of his parents, then by an alcoholic and un-motivated uncle, made him want to lash out on anyone or anything he could."

Mr. Taylor nodded in agreement.

"Well, he's at the Galloping G now," Roger said. "We'll just have to channel some of that energy and help him get back on track."

"That's the plan," Taylor said. "And since you seem to have it all under control, I'm going to take off. I'll give you a call to check on the boys in a few days."

Graham and Roger both shook hands with the probation officer. Then Roger walked him to his car.

"We'll be okay," her uncle said to Mr. Taylor. "Ryan needs a friend, and Jonah ain't as tough and unapproachable as he'd like us to believe."

"I think you're right," Taylor said as he climbed into his government-issued sedan. Moments later he drove away. His dust had barely settled when the boys returned.

"You want Ryan to help me finish up in the barn?" Jonah asked.

"It's probably a good idea if he had a tour of the ranch first," Graham said. "Think you can handle that?"

Jonah straightened his stance. "Sure, I can do it."

The screen door creaked open and slammed shut as Maddie came outside and approached the new boy with a grin. She took a moment to introduce herself; then she scanned him from head to toe, taking in his black cargo pants with a torn pocket and the black T-shirt with a picture of Chewbacca on the front.

She turned to Graham. "We're going to have to get him some real cowboy clothes, right?"

Sasha smiled. Leave it to Maddie to make sure everyone settled into ranch life—and quickly.

Graham reached for one of the girl's pigtails and gave it a gentle tug. "You're right, sweet pea. Looks like we'd better plan a shopping trip in Austin."

"I don't need anything," Ryan said.

"The minute one of those horses steps on your foot," Roger said, "you'll wish you were wearing boots."

The boy glanced down at his beat-up sneakers, which would be better off in a trash can than on a kid's feet.

He didn't need anything, huh?

Besides some new clothes and some meat on his bones, he was going to need plenty of kindness and understanding. He was also going to require a lot of guidance. Thank goodness he'd come to Peter's Place. He might have found himself in a lot more trouble if he hadn't.

"I gotta finish cleaning one more stall," Jonah said. "So I'll give him a tour as soon as I'm done."

"Good plan," Graham said. "I like the way you're taking your responsibilities seriously. And that you're determined to finish the job you started."

Jonah laughed. "Yeah, mucking stalls. Talk about *crappy* jobs."

Even the sad-faced Ryan smiled at the pun.

"But one reason I want to finish," Jonah added, "is

that it's Barney's stall. And he deserves to have it clean. So give me about five minutes."

After Jonah headed to the barn, Uncle Roger suggested that Maddie return to the kitchen to finish the chore he'd given her to do.

"Okeydoke," she said. "I like snappin' green beans." Then she dashed off.

Sasha took the opportunity to introduce herself to Ryan and to tell him she'd like to meet with him on a regular basis to talk about things.

"What kind of things?" he asked.

"Life—the past, the present, the future."

"I don't have much of a life or a future to think about, especially now. I made a really dumb mistake, and I'm sorry for messing with that equipment. But at least it got me out of my uncle's house."

"That might be true," she said. "But who were you punishing? Two years ago, you were thinking about college and could have been accepted by most of them. Now you've got time in juvie on your record."

Ryan frowned, then crossed his thin arms. "I was mad, okay? And I wanted everyone to know it."

"Mad or hurt?" she asked. "I lost my parents, too, so believe me, I know exactly how you feel."

"Do you?" The once-downcast kid straightened and stood as tall as his small stature would allow. "Did your parents leave a big insurance policy in trust for you so you could use it to go to college or buy a car or even a house someday? Did your uncle blow it all on drugs, hookers and booze?"

His words nearly knocked Sasha off-kilter, but she

rallied quickly. "I'd be as angry as hell, too, Ryan. But you're lashing out at the world, which isn't fair to anyone, especially you."

The teenager looked at her as if he was actually hearing and making sense of her words.

"You have an opportunity to turn everything around from this day forward," she added. "But changing the direction you're heading is a decision you have to make."

Ryan didn't say anything, but the cogs in his head appeared to be turning.

There was plenty of time to counsel him, but she suspected they'd taken a positive step forward already. Before any of them could comment, Jonah returned from the barn, brushing his dusty hands on his dirty, denim-clad thighs. "Okay, I'm done. I'll give you that tour now."

Ryan fell into step beside the bigger boy as they headed for the barn.

They were a sad pair, Sasha thought, although she had hope for both of them.

"I'd better check on Maddie," Roger said. "She might like snapping green beans, but she's probably already decided to quit on me."

As her uncle returned to the house, leaving Sasha and Graham standing in the yard, Sasha expected Graham to say he had to go back to work. Or maybe that he had to check on the teenagers. Either way, she figured he'd give her some reason he had to go. But he surprised her by remaining at her side.

He'd been avoiding her lately, so she was glad he hadn't made an excuse to skedaddle.

Before he opted to do just that, she decided to stretch out a little more time with him and asked, "So, what do you think?"

At the sound of Sasha's voice, Graham glanced up. He'd been so caught up in his musings about the boys and wondering how they'd do together that he'd probably missed something she'd said.

"What do I think about what?" he asked. "Ryan and the crime he committed?"

"Yes, that and whether you think he'll fit in here."

His biggest concern was how the boys would get along. Would they both be able to make some positive changes in their attitudes and their lives? Or would they hold each other back?

Graham lifted his Stetson, raked his fingers through his hair, then adjusted the hat back on his head. "Ryan's a smart kid. I think he'll do well here. And so will you."

She cocked her pretty head to the side. "Me? I'm not sure I'm following you."

The sunlight glistened on the white-blond strands of her hair, but he refused to let that distract him and explained what he'd meant. "I watched Ryan closely while you spoke to him. And I think he heard what you had to say. At least, he seemed to file away your comments."

"You really think so?"

Sasha had never lacked any confidence in the past, and the fact that she questioned herself now didn't sit well. He admired her manner, her way with the boys, although he didn't want to go overboard with his praise. It was too early to know how she'd do in the long run, although he suspected she'd be a natural.

"Yes, I liked what you told Ryan."

A smile claimed her renewed confidence. "Thank you. I thought it went over well, but you can never be sure, especially when talking to teenagers."

"That's true, but I think you nailed it. Ryan suffered one hell of a blow when his parents died, and I suspect he never had anyone to help him through it. Then, when his uncle damn near blew his plans for the future, he probably couldn't see any other way out of a bad situation."

Sasha nodded sagely. "You know, someone wise once told me that the essence of mental health is knowing that you have options. And Ryan has plenty of them, especially now that he's here."

She had a degree, but since she hadn't yet put it to use, Graham hadn't been entirely sure how she'd do working at Peter's Place. But after seeing her in action, first with Jonah and now with Ryan, he realized there wasn't any reason to hold any more interviews for an on-site counselor. Not when they already had Sasha.

"There's a home for delinquent teenagers in Austin," he said. "The setup isn't anything like this, but it might be a good idea if you took a look at it and maybe talked to the head counselor there. He might be able to help you develop your own program here."

"I'd like that." When she smiled, when her eyes lit up like that, it did something to him, something warm, something that skimmed his nerve endings and…

She folded her arms and rested them on her belly, reminding him of her condition and his inappropriate thoughts toward her. It also reminded him of her limitations. Maybe he ought to maintain that interview schedule after all.

"There's no hurry, though." He assumed she'd know what he meant. She wasn't going to be able to take on a full-time job for a while. He had no idea what restrictions her doctor had given her, although he had a sudden urge to find out and to make sure she took good care of herself and the baby. But did he have any right to pry?

They continued to stand in the yard in silence, but instead of thinking about the boys, as he'd done earlier, he studied Sasha and the way she bit down on her bottom lip, the way her brow furrowed. She was clearly pondering something serious.

Dang. Even concerned or worried, she was a lovely sight to behold. But he shook off his growing attraction.

"It might not be any of my business," he said, "but have you made an appointment with a local doctor yet?"

She looked up at him, those expressive blue eyes full of thoughts and emotions he had no idea how to read. "Are you worried about my pregnancy?"

As a matter of fact, yes. She appeared to be in good health, but he was still worried about her well-being— the baby's, too. And right this moment, everything about her concerned him. "When are you due?"

"August fifteenth."

That was about eight weeks away. His only experiences with labor and delivery involved broodmares. But this was different, *very* different.

"Just so you know," she said, "I have an appointment on Friday with an obstetrician in Austin."

"Good." That was a relief.

"I wouldn't let something that important lapse."

He didn't think she would. But he'd also heard that stress could bring on all sorts of physical ailments and complications for a pregnant woman. And Sasha must have suffered plenty of that over the past few months.

"I'd like to…" He paused, wishing he could recall what he'd been about to tell her. That he'd like to know what the new doctor had to say, he supposed. "I mean, I'm curious about that checkup, that's all."

"Do you want to go with me?" she asked.

Oh, hell no. He hadn't meant to be that forward or presumptuous. But then again, maybe that wasn't such a bad idea after all. But he was afraid to actually admit it.

"I could drive you there," he said. "I'd just hang out in the parking lot until you're finished. But that's up to you."

Damn. Now look at the can of worms he'd opened. That was another reason he needed to avoid her. It wasn't just the weird feelings she triggered in him whenever she was around; it was the crazy things he sometimes said.

"I must admit the drive from California was a bit difficult. My stomach is so big these days that I have to move the seat back so it doesn't rub against the steering wheel. And when I do that, my feet don't quite reach the gas or the brakes."

Graham had no idea how this conversation had actually unfolded, but he wasn't about to backpedal now. "I'd be happy to drive you to that appointment on Friday."

And for some wacky reason, he was even looking forward to it.

The next day, Graham showed up for breakfast in the ranch house, which not only surprised Sasha, but pleased her to no end.

"Good morning," she said. "You're just in time to have huevos rancheros."

"It tastes good, too," Jonah said. "So you better hurry up before me and Ryan eat it all."

Sasha glanced at the smaller boy, who'd just about cleaned his plate, which was a good sign, especially since Roger planned to "fatten him up" while he was here.

Jonah nudged Ryan with his elbow. "You like it, too. Don't you?"

Ryan stopped eating long enough to nod his agreement, the up-and-down motion causing his glasses to slip. He used his index finger to push them back on the bridge of his nose. She wondered who was in charge of taking him to an optometrist. The poor kid probably hadn't seen any doctors in a long while.

Roger, who stood at the stove filling a plate for Graham, chuckled. "I guess you finally got tired of fixing yourself a bowl of cold cereal every morning. I'm glad to hear it. Have a seat."

Graham didn't respond to the older man's comment. Instead he poured himself a cup of black coffee, took his plate and pulled out a chair next to Jonah.

"I like cold cereal sometimes," Maddie said. "Like today, when the food is hot and spicy and yucky."

Graham chuckled. "Your uncle is used to cooking for cowboys and sailors. I guess he forgot that little girls don't always like chilies and salsa."

Roger *hmph*ed. "I offer a variety of meals. We can't have silver-dollar hotcakes every morning. Besides, cereal isn't so bad, at least once in a while." He reached for the dishcloth and before wiping down the counter, added, "And just so all you ranch hands know, we're having my world-famous spaghetti for dinner tonight."

A slow grin stretched across Graham's face. "Now, that's what I call a treat. You can't believe how good Roger's meat sauce tastes. I'm tempted to join you guys."

And Sasha was tempted to steal Graham out of the kitchen, just so she could get him alone and tell him how she felt about him. But she knew better than that.

"By the way," Graham said, turning his attention to Maddie, "does your mom have any big plans for you today?"

The girl, who appeared delighted to be called on by the handsome cowboy, looked at Sasha. "Do you?"

"Not really." Sasha directed her question to Graham. "Why?"

"Because I think it's time to give Maddie another riding lesson."

At that, Maddie let out a squeal and clapped her hands. "I get to ride a horse again today?"

Graham took a sip of his coffee. When he lowered his mug, he grinned. "Sure. That is, if you're ready and it's okay with your mom."

"I'm ready right now." She pushed aside her plate and scooted her chair back.

Graham, his hero status in Maddie's eyes clearly growing by leaps and bounds, looked to Sasha for permission. But how could she possibly object? Maddie would ride every single day, from sunup to sundown if she could. But with as busy as the men had been, they hadn't had the time to supervise her. "Sure, it's fine with me."

"Good. Once I've finished eating breakfast and drinking my coffee, we'll go out and saddle Lady Jane."

Sasha's heart warmed at Graham's kindness toward her daughter. He'd already shown Maddie more attention in a couple of weeks than Gabe had in seven years. At least, when it came to quality time. That in itself was reason enough for Sasha to fall in love with him.

Well, maybe *love* wasn't the correct word. But it sure felt like the right one for what she was feeling.

Maddie carried her bowl of cereal, or rather the milk that remained, to the sink, where the boys would wash them after breakfast. Then she returned to her chair, placed her elbows on the table and plopped her chin upon her upturned hands as she proceeded to watch Graham eat, no doubt hoping he'd hurry.

Gabe would have found their daughter's behavior annoying and sent her away from the table. But it didn't seem to bother the rancher, who sported a big ol' grin stretched across his face.

A couple of minutes later, Graham finished his breakfast and carried his plate and empty coffee cup to the sink. "All right, sweet pea. I'm ready now. Does your mom want to watch?"

"You bet I do." Sasha wouldn't miss it for the world, and not just because she wanted to see her child taking part in an activity that made her so happy.

She followed Graham and Maddie outside, where the summer sun cast a glow on the ranch, mimicking the one that warmed her heart. When she spotted the bay mare that had been saddled and was waiting near the corral, she realized the lesson had been planned ahead of time.

"I love you," Maddie told the mare. "You're the best horse in the whole wide world."

Sasha smiled. If truth be told, Maddie had claimed to love the imaginary horse she'd made out of the sofa in the old house in which they'd once lived.

Graham lifted Maddie and placed her on the saddle. As the girl reached for the pommel, he adjusted the stirrups. Then he began to lead the mare around the yard. All the while, Maddie's bright-eyed smile couldn't get any larger.

Sasha wasn't sure how long her daughter's interest in horses and cowboys would last, but for now, you'd think Graham had offered her the moon.

As the back door creaked opened, she glanced over her shoulder to see Ryan and Jonah heading for the barn. The two chatted between themselves. Sasha might have been interested in what they had to say, but she was too intrigued by her daughter right now, by the pure joy on her face.

And she was far too caught up in all Graham had done for Maddie. Whatever she felt for him seemed to be growing stronger each day.

But where would that leave her and her family when he left?

Chapter Eight

Sasha had no more than locked the memory of Maddie's most recent riding lesson in her heart when her cell phone rang, putting a damper on what she'd thought of as a perfect day.

Before even looking at the lit display, she knew who was calling, and she'd been right. As much as she'd like to let the call go to voice mail, she answered, anyway. But that didn't ensure an upbeat tone when she said, "Hello, Gabe."

"Hey," her soon-to-be ex-husband said. "How're things going out there?"

It was nice that he cared enough to ask. She and Maddie had always been at the lower end of his priority list. But at least he'd followed up on his promise to call her after she'd had gotten settled at the ranch. "We're fine, Gabe. How about you?"

"Busy—as usual."

That was typical. Gabe had begun to build a life of his own way before the two of them separated. He'd blamed it on his adventurous spirit, something she'd found exciting and appealing when she met him during her freshman year in college. But over time, she'd realized that, in reality, he'd been a restless soul, a tumbleweed who rolled along from one interest or job to another.

"So, what's new?" she asked.

"For one thing, I was talking to my parents the other day."

Now, *that* was unusual. He'd never been especially close to his father. Or to his mother, for that matter. And for that reason alone, neither she nor Maddie had ever really bonded with his parents, not in the way she'd once hoped and imagined they would.

She wondered if they'd been upset by the divorce. If so, neither of them had taken the time to call her and ask how she was faring, how she was feeling. Was she wrong to think that was odd?

"How are they doing?" she asked.

"Actually, they're doing okay. Now, anyway. My mom found a breast lump a while back, something she hadn't wanted to bother me with. She's undergoing treatment but seems to be okay. And Dad had a minor heart attack last week."

"I'm sorry to hear that."

"Yeah. Me, too. So I figured it might be time for me to take my dad up on his offer to work for the family corporation."

Finally? It had taken two serious health issues for Gabe to see the wisdom in that? It was a good move for him and his father, but she wondered how long that would last. "I'm sure your dad will be happy to hear about your decision."

"I already told him, and he was. Anyway, my mom asked about our plans for the holidays."

"*Our* plans?"

"She wanted us—or rather me—to bring the girls for Christmas."

Sasha had assumed they'd be with her. In the eight years she and Gabe had been married, they'd only spent the holidays with his parents a couple of times.

"I know I've never been big on family celebrations or gatherings," he said. "But I'm turning over a new leaf."

She bit back a sarcastic response and tamped down her anger. Why hadn't he thought about doing that years ago when there'd still been hope for their marriage?

Instead she said, "I'm glad to hear that." And for Maddie's sake, she hoped it wasn't just another passing fancy.

"My mom wants to have an old-fashioned Christmas this year. She'd like to have Maddie help her to bake cookies and that sort of thing. I know it's early to be making plans this far in advance, but I thought we should start thinking about that, along with a visitation schedule."

"I suppose you can have Maddie on Christmas Eve," Sasha said. "But I want her on Christmas Day."

"Fair enough. I'll take her home to you in the morning."

She hadn't yet told him that she planned to stay in

Texas, but now wasn't the time. She'd prefer to wait until all the paperwork was signed and filed with the court. Besides, the holidays were still five or six months away.

Sasha's only response was to blow out a wobbly sigh.

"But what about…um…the baby?" he asked.

The "um…baby" had a name. She'd told him several times that she'd planned to call her Sydney, but apparently he'd forgotten.

"What about her?" Sasha asked.

"Mom wants her to come, too."

Sasha's heart dropped to the pit of her stomach. There was no way she'd let Gabe take an infant for an overnight visit, and she was surprised he'd even suggested it.

Maddie had been a fussy, challenging baby who'd required much of Sasha's time. And Gabe had avoided being around her every chance he got. If Sasha wanted to stir up a fight, she'd remind Gabe how resentful he'd been—and not just because of the noise. He hadn't liked taking second place, even to his daughter. So it was difficult to believe that their girls were becoming more important to him.

"I'm sorry," Sasha said. "I don't feel right about letting you take the baby for more than an hour. She'll only be a few months old, and I plan to breast-feed."

"I understand that. And believe me, I know how tough it is when babies get fussy. But my mom will help out. Won't you agree for her?"

Sasha had never held anything against Gabe's mother, although Claire Smith been so caught up with her bridge group, her golf friends and her charity work that she'd never made her family a huge priority, either. However, facing one's mortality would cause one to re-evaluate life and make changes.

Hopefully, Gabe was actually planning to make a few changes himself. And wouldn't that be good for the kids?

Yes, it would. And she actually appreciated that.

But how would a visit to California impact her first holiday season on the Galloping G? She hadn't shared a Christmas dinner with Uncle Roger in… Well, she couldn't remember when. And she'd planned to make a big deal out of decorating the tree, hanging stockings and baking with Maddie.

And then there was Graham…

Oh, for Pete's sake. Who knew where he'd be by then? Hadn't he told her he'd be moving to Austin in the near future?

"I don't know," she said. "I need some time to think about it. In the meantime, would you consider celebrating with your family the weekend before or after the holiday?"

"If that's the only way you'll agree, then maybe we'd better do it earlier. I think my mom is going to kick the cancer, but…well, you never know."

As much as Sasha would like to hold on to her resentment and to prohibit Gabe from seeing the children at all, especially overnight, she couldn't do that legally. And even if she could, she wouldn't. Neither would she prevent his parents from seeing their grandchildren.

"We'll work something out," she said.

"Good. I'd appreciate that. It might be nice if you

and the girls joined us for Thanksgiving, too. It would make my mom really happy."

Well, it wouldn't make Sasha happy. She'd had enough of those awkward family dinners, when Gabe and his father would often have words, then lapse into silence. And the fact that their divorce would be final by then would only make things more nerve-racking, more strained.

"Let's talk about this later," she said. "By the way, is Mr. Stanley back in town?" She and her attorney had suggested a change in their agreement, but Ron Stanley, Gabe's lawyer, had been on vacation when she left town.

"I have no idea. Like I said, I've been swamped with one thing or another. I guess I'd better call his office and ask."

She wished she could believe him. He'd always been one to downplay the seriousness of a situation, especially if it mattered to her. "Please call today. I don't want to prolong this thing. And you're a born procrastinator."

"Is there some reason you need the divorce to be finalized immediately?"

Graham came to mind. But she was dreaming again.

"Yes," she said. "I'd like to put it behind me for good."

"Sheesh, Sasha. It's pretty obvious you've been talking to your uncle. That crusty old man has a mean streak and hasn't ever liked me."

She had the urge to sling her cell phone across the room. How dare Gabe blame any of their problems on Uncle Roger?

"I don't want to fight with you," she said. "Just follow through on your part of the agreement in a timely manner, and I'll do the same."

"Don't worry. I'll take care of things on my end. And after I do, maybe I'll come out there to visit."

Seriously? He'd never wanted to before, and she'd asked several times. The thought of him showing up on the Galloping G unsettled her.

When the call ended, she still felt compelled to wind up and let the phone fly. Instead she swore under her breath and turned away, only to see Uncle Roger in the doorway.

Did he realize who she'd been talking to? A scowl on his face suggested he did. And if that was the case, he'd probably stood in the doorway long enough to have heard plenty.

He closed the gap between them and crossed his arms. "What did that…guy have to say?"

"Not much. He just wanted to ask how Maddie was doing." Sasha offered up a smile, hoping her uncle hadn't sensed her frustration and worries.

He let out a *hmph*, but his expression mellowed, which indicated he'd accepted her explanation.

Thank goodness for that. No matter how badly she'd like to share her mounting fears with someone, Roger didn't need any more reasons to dislike Gabe.

Besides, if Gabe showed up on the Galloping G as he'd said he might, she didn't want her ex-husband and her uncle coming to blows.

The afternoon sun slipped down in the western sky as Graham and the boys continued to work on the downed fence. It would have been fixed already if Roger would have used the insurance money to hire professionals to do it. But he and Graham had decided it would be a good project for the boys. They'd actually made a surprising amount of progress so far, especially since each of the teenagers seemed determined to outwork the other.

If truth be told, they were both doing a fine job, even Ryan, who'd yet to bulk up or put on that much-needed weight.

A hammer pounded on wood, followed by a boy's voice crying out a string of obscenities. Graham turned away from the post he'd been centering to see Jonah gripping his left hand while jumping up and down.

He didn't need to ask what happened, although he probably ought to assess the injury.

"He got his thumb instead of the nail," Ryan said.

Graham nodded, then made his way to the bigger boy. "Let me see."

"I think…I busted it." He grimaced and swore again. "Thank goodness this isn't my pitching arm. But damn, it hurts like hell."

As soon as Jonah was willing to unlock his grip, Graham checked out his thumb. He'd caught the tip of it. The nail was already turning black and blue, and he would eventually lose it.

"I think it's just a bad bruise," Graham said. "But if you want me to take you to the Urgent Care for an X-ray, I can. Either way, let's call it a day. We've already gotten more work done than I expected us to."

Jonah glanced at Ryan, then back at Graham. "I don't need to see a doctor."

"The offer stands. In the meantime, let's go to the house and put some ice on it."

The boy swore again for good measure, then muttered, "Whatever."

Once back at the house, they found Sasha in the kitchen. She'd just brewed a gallon jar of sun tea. When she turned around and offered them a glass, she noticed Jonah holding his wrist.

"Uh-oh." Sasha was by the boy's side instantly, gauging the seriousness of the injury. "What happened?"

Graham folded his arms across his chest. "He had a run-in with a hammer."

"That's a nasty bruise," she said. "And it's swelling. I'll get some ice."

Ryan, who stood to the side, observing Sasha's efforts to render first aid, made his way to Graham. "There's still a couple hours of daylight left. You want me to do anything?"

"No, you can go back to your room, shower and rest up for dinner."

"Maybe I should go see about the horses," Ryan said. "I could give them carrots or an apple or something."

"Good idea." Graham reached into the fruit bowl on the counter and removed two red apples. "There's a paring knife in the cupboard next to the left of the sink. Take it with you."

As Ryan proceeded to do as he was told, Graham added, "Just don't cut yourself. I only allow one accident per day."

Ryan smiled, a rare reaction but a good one. "Got it, boss."

Sasha set a bowl of ice water on the table in front of Jonah, then took a seat beside him and watched as he soaked his sore thumb.

She was wearing a white T-shirt and a pair of snug-fitting blue jeans, nothing fancy. But she looked especially pretty today. She'd pulled her hair up into a messy topknot, revealing a pair of diamond studs in her delicate earlobes.

Graham wondered if Gabe had given the dazzling earrings to her. He wouldn't be surprised. Sasha was the kind of woman Graham would shower with gifts. And expensive ones, at that.

"I hope this doesn't screw up my mobility," Jonah said.

Graham knew he wasn't just referring to dexterity. The kid loved baseball, and according to that report Brad Taylor had shared, he was a good player.

Before Graham could bring up the subject, Sasha did it for him. "That reminds me, Jonah. I asked around and found out the name of our local high school baseball coach. I know the season is over, but there's always next year. I know Mr. Atwater would like to meet you. What would you say if I invited him out to the ranch someday?"

Jonah's jaw dropped, his once-surly attitude nowhere in sight. "No kidding? You'd invite the coach here?"

"Sure," Sasha said. "I've heard you've got one heck of a pitching arm."

The boy shrugged. "I'm pretty good. At least, I used to be when there was someone to play with. But are you saying there's actually a chance I could attend the high school instead of taking classes here with Mrs. McCrea? And that I might even get to play ball again?"

"I can't see why not. If you continue to work hard and promise not to get into any trouble, I think we could work that out." Sasha glanced at Graham. "Don't you agree?"

"We'll talk to Mrs. McCrea and see what she thinks about a transfer."

"You won't be sorry," Jonah said. "I'll work my ass off this summer. And I'll keep out of trouble. I promise."

He studied his hand—not the one with the bum thumb, but the one he used for pitching fastballs and curves. He turned it one way, then the other, opening and flexing his fingers.

It was a shame he'd had to give up baseball before, but it was an even bigger shame that he'd acted out and gotten into trouble.

Sasha placed her forearms on the table and leaned forward. "You know, if you really want to punish someone by your rebellion, you might try channeling it in a way that it won't hurt you."

"What do you mean?" Jonah asked.

"I might be wrong, but I have a feeling you blame your father for bailing out on you and your family."

"Damn straight. It's all his fault."

"But the only ones you hurt when you got into trouble were your mom and yourself."

The boy lowered his head and scrunched his forehead, but he neither agreed nor offered up a defense.

"Unfortunately, your dad left your mom in dire

straits financially. So she was forced to work two jobs to feed you and your younger brothers and sisters. She needed someone's help, and that someone was you."

Jonah looked up and caught Sasha's gaze. "I let her down. I know. But dang, she let me down, too."

"How?" Sasha asked.

"I don't know. Maybe she shouldn't have spent all her time at work and then paid more attention to the younger kids than she did to me."

"Whoa," Graham said. "I think it's admirable that your mom did everything she could to hold the family together. And she probably wasn't able to give anyone the time they deserved, so she focused on the ones who needed her most."

"Yeah. I know. But…" The boy pursed his lips and held back his thoughts, something he wouldn't have done the first day he arrived.

"I know it feels as if your mom set out to hurt or punish you," Sasha said, "but I doubt that's the case."

His shoulders drooped. "Yeah, I know. But it wasn't fair."

"Maybe not. And I'm sure that she's now wishing that she'd done things differently when you were at home. I know that's the way I feel when I mess up. But for the record, life *isn't* always fair. Sometimes a person you thought you could lean on or depend upon will wimp out and not follow through on his or her obligations. And that means someone else has to become the responsible one."

The boy didn't respond, but he seemed to be pondering her words. Graham was pondering them, too.

She had to be speaking from personal experience, but Jonah had no way of knowing that.

Sasha fell silent. When she glanced at Graham, a smile flickered across her lips. He winked at her, letting her know that he'd not only agreed with her, but had caught on to what she'd implied.

As their gazes locked, silently binding them together once again, all those weird, inexplicable feelings he'd been having tumbled around in his chest, threatening to trip him up—if he'd let them. But he couldn't think about that now.

Instead he thought about the kind of social worker and counselor Sasha was going to make. The boys who stayed on the ranch were going to be lucky to have her here.

Graham ought to be comforted by the fact that things would run smoothly at Peter's Place, even when he was gone. And in a way, he did feel better.

Only trouble was, the plans he had to start his own business in the city no longer seemed quite so pressing. And he wasn't in any big rush to leave.

On Friday morning, as promised, Graham drove Sasha into Austin for her doctor's appointment. They didn't talk much on the way. For one thing, he wasn't quite sure what to say to her. Other than friendship, there wasn't much he could offer. At least, that was all until her divorce was finalized.

He hadn't planned to ask, but the question rolled off his tongue without a thought to whether it was appropriate or not. "Are you and Gabe just separated? Or have you actually filed for divorce?"

"The paperwork has been filed, although there's an amendment that needs to be made. Why?"

Because he wondered just how invested she was in her marriage. Would she be open to a reconciliation if the opportunity arose? And if not, when would she be free so he could... Do what? Pursue her himself?

"I was just wondering," he said.

A mile down the road, he looked across the seat where she sat, staring out the window at the passing scenery.

Curiosity prompted him to question her again. "When will it be final?"

"I don't know. Soon, I think."

He hoped so—for her sake. Okay, and maybe for his own sake, too. He stole another glance at her, watched her place her hand over her ever-expanding baby bump.

Was she worried about her upcoming doctor's appointment? Did she wish she still had a husband to go through pregnancy and childbirth with her?

Graham knew a couple of guys who'd actually gone to obstetrical appointments with their pregnant wives, but he wasn't the father of Sasha's baby. So it still surprised him that he'd not only volunteered to go with her, but that he'd also considered asking if he could go in the exam room with her.

It was weird, though. He would've thought that he'd feel uncomfortable to even consider something like that, but for some reason, he didn't.

Truth be told, if she asked him to, he'd probably agree. But why would she ask? She'd never given him any reason to think she'd want him there.

After parking his pickup, he remained behind the wheel and turned in his seat. "Do you want me to wait for you out here? Or should I go inside?"

She tucked a strand of hair behind her ear. "I have no idea how long I'll be, and it could get warm out here. Why don't you come in with me?"

He figured she meant he should come as far as the waiting room, which was probably best. So he opened the driver's door and got out. Once she slid out of the passenger seat and he locked the vehicle, he walked with her to the entrance. He pushed open the glass door for her, then they proceeded to the elevator.

"It's on the third floor," she said, pushing the proper button to take them up.

When the elevator doors opened, they stepped out and walked along the hallway until they found 302. Again, he opened the door and followed her inside. While she signed in at the front desk, he removed his Stetson and scanned the waiting area. He spotted a couple of empty chairs and pointed them out to her when she returned.

Sasha took a seat, leaving the one next to her for him. She'd no more than settled into the chair when she whispered, "I've heard great things about this doctor."

"I'm glad. It's nice to know you'll in good hands."

Moments later, a tall, dark-complexioned man in his late thirties or early forties entered the room. He checked out the empty chairs before taking the seat next to Graham. Moments later, he snatched a *Parents* magazine from the table beside him and began to thumb through it.

Graham wondered where the guy's wife was. Had she been called back to see the doctor already? Was she going to meet him here?

Not that it mattered. He looked at the magazine offerings: *Good Housekeeping, Baby Talk*... Nothing he found especially appealing.

He wasn't sure how long they'd have to wait. After all, a lot of doctors didn't run on time. But he was here for the long haul.

Several minutes later, a woman wearing pink scrubs called Sasha's name.

"Oh, good," she said, getting to her feet. "I shouldn't be too long, but who knows?"

Apparently, she didn't want him to go in with her, which was her call. "No problem. I'll be here."

Sasha nodded, then grabbed her purse and headed toward the smiling nurse in the doorway.

Once she'd disappeared behind the door that led to the exam rooms, the man next to him leaned toward him. "First baby?"

"Uh, no. I'm just a friend of the mother's. How about you?"

"Yep. First-time dad here." A smile stretched across his face, lighting his brown eyes. "My wife and I tried for years to have a baby on our own, but we didn't have any luck. So we're adopting a baby that will be born around Thanksgiving, and now we're going to really be parents."

"Congratulations."

"Thanks." The man set his magazine aside. "You have no idea how happy we are—or how excited I am to be able to attend the OB appointments. In fact, I'm supposed to meet my wife and the birth mom here in about forty-five minutes."

Graham smiled. "You're early."

"Yep. That's how eager I am for this appointment. We're supposed to have an ultrasound today, and we're hoping to find out if we're going to have a boy or girl."

"That's cool," Graham said, surprisingly happy for the guy.

"Yep. It's not every day that you get to meet your own son or daughter. And I couldn't care less that we don't have the same DNA. Anyone can be a sperm donor, right? But it takes a special man to be a dad."

Graham knew exactly what the guy meant. His own father had kids all over the world, but he hadn't actually raised some of them.

A sperm donor, huh? That about sized it up, he supposed.

He thought about Sasha, about her daughters. Gabe Smith had supplied those girls with his DNA and was their legal father, but was he going to actually step up and take a loving, parental role with them, especially now that they lived out of state?

From what Roger had said and Graham had gathered, it wasn't likely. Gabe Smith might not be "special" enough to be a real dad. So who would man up and be there for those girls—and for their pretty mom?

Graham?

The idea of assuming that kind of responsibility ought to scare the hell out of him. But for some reason, he thought he might be up to the task.

Chapter Nine

After her exam, Sasha stopped by the reception desk and scheduled her next appointment to see the obstetrician for two weeks from today. Then she returned to the waiting room, where she'd left Graham.

When he spotted her, he took his hat from the table in front of him, got to his feet and ambled toward her. "So, how did it go? Is everything okay?"

"It went very well. They already have my medical records, so that made for an easy transition."

"Good. Do you like the new doctor?"

"Yes, I do. She has a nice way about her and really seems to know her stuff."

"That's got to be a relief." Graham opened the door for her, and they stepped into the corridor that led to the elevator.

Sasha had worried about changing doctors in mid-stream, but once she'd made up her mind to start a new life without Gabe, she hadn't wanted to wait until after she'd recovered from childbirth to move to Texas.

When they reached the elevator, Graham hit the down button.

"So the baby's doing all right?" He glanced at her belly, and a crooked grin tickled his lips. "From the looks of it, she certainly seems to be growing."

Sasha rested her hands over her expanding baby bump, glad to know little Sydney was healthy. Yet, as a result, she herself had become bigger and more cumbersome. But there wasn't much she could do about that.

"Everything is right on track," she said. "I should deliver in a little over six weeks."

The elevator doors opened, and Graham let Sasha enter first. Considering how happy she was to have him by her side, she ought to glide into the car, her feet on little clouds. Instead she waddled like a plump, well-fed Christmas goose.

Once Graham had joined her, they descended to the lobby.

"If there's anything I can do…" He paused, then shrugged. "I mean, if there's anything you need, just say the word."

A friendly face and a hand to hold during labor would be nice, but she'd gotten by without either last time. She'd told herself that Gabe would have been there if he hadn't come down with the flu. Since Maddie had decided to make her entrance two weeks early and Gabe's parents had been on a golf vacation in Hawaii at the time, Sasha hadn't had anyone to coach or support her through it all.

That was all behind her now, but still, it would be comforting to know someone would sit by her side when baby Sydney entered the world. As much as Sasha loved Uncle Roger, he'd probably be more helpful if he drank coffee in the hospital cafeteria and waited until he got word that it was all over.

She shot a glance at Graham. Could she...?

No, if she broached a question like that with him, he'd probably balk at her audacity, which would ruin their budding friendship. So she kept that thought to herself as they left the medical building and crossed the parking lot.

When they reached the spot where Graham had left his pickup, he asked, "So, now what? Do you have any shopping you need to do?"

"I'd rather do that next time I'm in Austin. I want to check on Maddie. Plus, I have a couple of calls I need to make."

"All right." Graham circled to the passenger side of the pickup, pushed the unlock button on the remote and opened the door for her.

How sweet—and gallant. Just like a knight in shining armor. Again she was struck by how handsome he was, how kind. And how very different he was from Gabe.

But she couldn't very well pursue anything romantic with him at this point. So she slid into her seat, blowing out a soft sigh of resignation as she did.

After Graham started the engine and backed out of the parking lot, they headed to the ranch.

"Thanks for driving me," she said.

"You're welcome. I'd be happy to do it again for your next appointment."

"I'd appreciate that." And she would. In fact, she'd better start focusing on the future and the positive changes that had occurred since she'd left California.

As difficult as it was going to be to go through labor and delivery, and then raise two daughters on her own, she had a lot to be grateful for and should count her blessings. After all, she had Maddie, Uncle Roger... and now Graham, who was proving to be a good friend.

She just wished that someday he'd become more than that.

That night, after the boys ate dinner and returned to their cabin to do the homework assignments their teacher had given them, Uncle Roger volunteered to read a bedtime story to Maddie.

"Only one?" Maddie cocked her head to the side. "I brought some really, really good books from home. Maybe you could read all of them to me."

Roger chuckled. "Sure. Why not?"

As Maddie took her great-uncle by the hand to lead him to her bedroom and the books she'd stacked next to her closet door, Sasha told them she'd be back shortly. Then she stepped out the front door, crossed the yard and went to Graham's cabin.

Ever since she first arrived on the Galloping G, she'd been tempted to visit him so they could talk privately. But other than delivering a meal now and then, she hadn't been able to come up with an excuse that was good enough. But she had one now.

After she'd arrived home from her doctor's appointment, she called the local high school, which was open to kids needing to take remedial courses during the summer. She hoped to connect with someone who could relate to the boys and their interests.

Chuck Atwater, the baseball coach, wasn't at work, but Caroline Stewart, the head of the science department, was. So Sasha had told her about Peter's Place and the boys who had recently come to live here.

Mrs. Stewart seemed genuinely interested in Ryan, especially when Sasha mentioned his interest in science and math, his tragic past and the trouble he'd gotten into.

"I'd be more than happy to talk to him," the teacher had said.

When Sasha had told her about Jonah and his interest in baseball, she said she'd get in contact with Coach Atwater. So things were coming together nicely.

She hadn't set a date for the teachers from the high school to visit the ranch, since she'd wanted to talk it over with Graham first. So that was what she planned to do now.

After climbing the steps to his cabin, she lifted her hand and knocked.

Graham answered the door wearing only a pair of worn jeans. The sight of him bare-chested almost knocked her to her knees.

Sure, she'd noted his broad shoulders, muscular chest

and bulging biceps before, but she hadn't been prepared for those taut abs.

Under normal circumstances, it would have been easy to focus on his sparkling blue eyes and gorgeous face. But that was when he was fully dressed in all his cowboy glory—and not when he was obviously ready for bed and sexier than ever.

"I…uh…" She couldn't seem to form a single word, let alone a greeting. But that didn't matter. He appeared to be just as surprised to see her.

"Hey!" A crooked grin tugged at his lips. "I thought you might be one of the boys."

"I'm sorry. I didn't realize it was so late." She glanced over her shoulder, at the path she'd taken, wishing she hadn't come. "You know, what I had to say really wasn't that important. I can talk to you tomorrow, maybe at breakfast."

"It's not late, and I wasn't asleep. Come on in." He swung open the door and stepped aside so she could enter the small quarters he called home. It was a modest abode for a man related to the Robinson and Fortune clans.

Sasha hadn't been in one of the Galloping G cabins for years, and certainly not this one, with its small stone fireplace and open-beamed ceiling. The wooden floor was dotted with several colorful throw rugs that looked fairly new.

Graham didn't have much furniture, just a leather sofa, a rustic lamp with a cowhide shade and a television mounted on a wall bracket. He'd been watching a sports channel, the volume on low.

A dark oak coffee table held a TV remote and a long-neck beer bottle, resting on a folded napkin he'd used as a makeshift coaster.

Graham picked up the remote and shut off the TV and the ball game he'd been watching.

"Have a seat," he said, indicating the sofa, which was her only option. That meant they'd be sitting side by side.

She brushed her palms, which suddenly seemed a bit clammy, along the fabric of her sundress and bit down on her bottom lip. Dang, what on earth had she been thinking when she came to talk to him this evening? Her mind was swirling with all kinds of inappropriate thoughts and scenarios that couldn't possibly play themselves out. She ought to make an excuse to leave before things got any more awkward, but she did her best to shake off her insecurity and sat down.

"So, what's up?" he asked.

Right. Her actual reason for coming to talk to him. "I placed a call to the high school today and spoke to one of the teachers about Peter's Place and the boys."

"Good idea. What did they say? Were they concerned about having a 'bad' element infiltrate their campus?"

"Well, I'm sure that crossed their minds, although it's a public school and I think they have to take them." She tucked a strand of hair behind her ear. "I told her we already had a teacher working here and that we'd only send the boys to the high school if they were ready to mainstream into a regular classroom situation."

"How did that explanation go over with them?"

"Actually, very well. I spoke to Caroline Stewart,

the head of the science department and the one who teaches a couple of AP classes. I told her about Ryan's potential, and she'd like to meet him."

"That's great." Graham stretched out his bare arm along the back of the sofa.

"I thought I'd invite her out to see the ranch and to meet the boys next weekend. Hopefully, she can bring Chuck Atwater, the baseball coach. He's not working at the school this summer, but Caroline said he's looking for new talent for next season."

"Wow, you've been busy—and productive. I'm impressed." A broad smile and a glimmer in his eyes convinced her that he wasn't just blowing smoke. He truly valued her efforts.

Just knowing that he admired her touched something deep inside, something that yearned to be appreciated, to be needed.

Graham, whose arm still stretched along the sofa's backrest, shifted in his seat, his fingers moving closer to her shoulder.

Focus on his eyes, Sasha.

"Was Mrs. Stewart apprehensive about the trouble the boys got into?" he asked.

"Somewhat, I think. But I explained that Ryan's primary purpose in damaging that equipment was to get himself removed from his uncle's home."

"Did Ryan actually come out and admit that?" Graham asked.

"Not in so many words, but I'm sure of it."

Graham's finger was dangling by her shoulder. She

tried not to think about how easily he could touch her—
if he were so inclined.

"What made you decide to be a social worker?" he
asked.

Good question. She needed to keep the conversation
on track. "When I was in the Girl Scouts, our troop
would sometimes work along with a sorority that took
on service projects. A couple of times we served meals
to the homeless. We were also included in other projects to help people who were struggling to make ends
meet. And that's when I decided I'd like to do that kind
of work when I grew up."

"You have a big heart."

"I guess so, especially for those who aren't as fortu-
nate as I am." She turned in her seat, facing him. "You
know, losing my mom and dad was tough, but I had loving grandparents and, of course, Uncle Roger to help me
through it. I never had to worry about where I'd sleep at
night or when I'd get my next meal. A lot of people—
and sadly, way too many children—aren't that lucky."

"That's why I'm glad we can help some of those
kids here."

We? She smiled at the thought of being Graham's
teammate. She liked it—a lot.

"It's amazing what love, kindness and understanding can do," she said.

"You've got a real gift, Sasha. I heard you talk to
both Ryan and Jonah. You're able to relate to them. So
becoming a counselor is a good career move for you."

"I've wanted to work with kids for a long time. After
Peter died, I was devastated. So my grandparents sent

me to counseling. The experience was a good one, and I took courses in psychology and social work when I was in college. The rest is history."

"I'm so proud of the woman you've become." He trailed his fingers along her upper arm, radiating heat to her shoulder and setting off a rush of tingles that nearly unraveled her at the seams.

What was going on? Why had he touched her like that? Did she dare read something into it?

The emotion glowing in his eyes warmed her heart in such an unexpected way that she forgot her momentary concern and pretended, just for a moment, that something romantic was brewing between them.

She tossed him a playful grin. "I'm glad to hear you say that, especially when you once thought of me as a pest."

"Yeah, well, I wish I'd known then who the woman that little girl was going to grow up to be. Things might have been…"

His words drifted off, but her heart soared at the implication. Might he have given her the time of day? Might he have developed feelings for her?

As she searched his expression, looking for an answer, their gazes locked. A bolt of something powerful snapped and crackled in the silence, until he pulled his hand away and muttered, "Dammit."

"What's the matter?" she asked, although she feared what he might say.

"This is a real struggle for me, Sasha."

She had a wild thought that he actually might be attracted to her, but she was crazy to even consider it for a moment. Yet she waited to hear him out, bracing herself for disappointment.

He merely studied her as if she ought to know just what he was talking about. But she couldn't be sure. And she'd be darned if she'd read something nonexistent into it.

He raked his fingers through his hair, mussing it in a way she found appealing.

"I'm feeling things for you that I have no right to feel," he admitted.

The revelation stunned her, pleased her. Thrilled her. And she found it difficult to think, to respond.

"Seriously?"

He slowly shook his head. "I'm afraid so. And I'm sorry, especially since you still belong to another man."

Sasha hadn't "belonged" to anyone in a long time, and if truth be told, the only man she wanted to belong to was Graham. But she was still afraid to make any assumptions about what he was saying.

"For what it's worth," she said, "I might still be legally married, but I won't be for long. The divorce will be final soon."

"I'll have to wait to ask you out until then."

Graham wanted to date her? Her surprise must have been splashed all over her face, because he asked, "Does that shock you?"

"Yes, it does. To be honest, I had a humongous crush on you when I was younger."

"Really?" A slow grin stretched across his face. "You never told me."

"I knew you weren't interested back then. So it's kind

of nice to know you…like me now." Could she have downplayed her feelings for him any more than that?

"So you're not opposed to going out with me?" he asked.

If she weren't still legally married and seven months pregnant, she might have insisted that they go out right now. But she was afraid to jinx things, to lose Graham before she'd actually won him.

Sure, he'd kissed her before. But he'd apologized afterward. What was she supposed to think?

"I can't believe you actually want to date me," she said.

"You can believe it. I'd actually like to do more than just that."

As if his words hadn't thoroughly jerked the rug out from under her, he slid across the seat and slipped his arms around her in a move that was more than persuading.

As their lips met, hers parted, allowing him full access to her mouth. His tongue sought hers, and the kiss intensified until she had no doubt about what he meant, what he felt.

Could this really be happening? Should she risk telling him how badly she'd wanted this, wanted him?

Not when she was afraid to blink—or to pinch herself. Dang, if she was dreaming, she didn't want to wake up.

Savoring his taste, his musky scent, she lifted her hand and placed it on his bare chest, felt his body heat, the whisper of hair on his skin, the steady beat of his heart.

She probably should put a stop to this. Shouldn't she? Yet she really wasn't legally or emotionally bound to Gabe any longer. Besides, their marriage had been a sham for years.

Whether it was right or wrong, Sasha continued to kiss Graham for all she was worth. But just as she felt herself weaken, as she felt compelled to spill out all her romantic thoughts, he drew back.

"I'm sorry," he said. "I don't want to hurt you or the baby."

She doubted he'd hurt either of them. After all, the doctor hadn't said anything about abstaining from sex. But she was so caught up in his admission, in his unselfish concern for her and her child, that she didn't press the issue or encourage him to throw caution to the wind.

So she said, "All right."

She feared he might get up at that point, ending the tender romantic moment, but he drew her closer. As she leaned into him and settled into his embrace, she felt truly loved and cared for in the first time since…well, forever, it seemed.

Yet the idea of trusting Graham with her heart scared her to death.

What would she do if he tired of her, a fussy infant and a precocious little girl? What if this dream come true ended before it even got started?

Not that she thought Graham lacked commitment. Look at all he'd done to help Uncle Roger with the ranch, with Peter's Place. He'd also been mentoring Jonah and Ryan.

But there was something else that caused her concern—

his refusal to work at Robinson Tech. After all, families were important. And while she admired all he'd done on the Galloping G, she worried he might walk away from her if the going got tough.

Just as Gabe had.

As Graham rested his head against Sasha's, he relished the feel of her in his arms and the light scent of her peach-blossom fragrance. The heated kiss they'd shared, as well as the memory of the first one, convinced him that what he'd been feeling for her was the real deal.

There was no longer any doubt in his mind that he wanted her, and he was determined to make the three of them—rather, the *four* of them—a real family.

He had to admit that becoming an overnight father would be a big change for him, but he adored Maddie. And he was already feeling something for the little one Sasha carried, the baby who was due to be born in six short weeks.

He could open his heart and tell that to Sasha now. In fact, he probably should, but she might not be ready to hear something that heavy, especially when she was still reeling emotionally from her split with Gabe.

Still, she'd agreed to date him, which was a big step in the right direction.

He'd like to ask her to stay the night with him, to just lie next to him and cuddle. But she couldn't do that. He supposed he'd have to be content to hold her like this for as long as she'd let him.

A moment later, she said, "I probably ought to go back to the house. It's past Maddie's bedtime."

He understood why she had to go. "Tell her good-night for me."

"I will." Yet she didn't make a move toward leaving. And he didn't remove his arm from her shoulders.

He sensed that she had something on her mind, words she wanted to say, yet didn't.

If so, what was she holding back?

And why?

Did she still have feelings for her ex? Graham sure hoped that wasn't the case. And for more reasons than the obvious. Gabe Smith didn't deserve her or their daughters.

"I don't want you to keep Maddie waiting," he said. "But for the record, I could sit like this all night."

"Me, too."

Truthfully? Did she still harbor any remnants of the crush she'd once had on him, the one he hadn't been aware of? He hoped so, because he'd meant what he'd said about liking the woman she'd grown into. Of course, that wasn't exactly right. He *loved* the woman she'd become.

Either way, he didn't want to scare her off. So he was determined to keep his feelings under wraps, to be patient and take it slow and easy.

It seemed like the best plan to him. And one he didn't think would backfire.

On Sunday morning, when Mrs. Stewart and Coach Atwater came to visit the ranch, Graham and Sasha met them outside before introducing them to the boys. If Graham ever had a reason to respect the teaching profession, it was after seeing these two in action.

Chuck Atwater, a tall, lanky man in his late forties or early fifties, wore a pair of jeans and a black T-shirt with a brightly colored superhero logo. Graham had to do a double take because the laid-back guy with a receding hairline didn't look like a coach. At least, he didn't resemble any of those Graham used to have.

And Caroline Stewart, who was much younger and more stylish than he'd thought the head of the high school science department would be, surprised him, too. He'd been expecting to see a female geek. But apparently, he'd been watching too many episodes of *The Big Bang Theory*.

Nevertheless, he and Sasha gave them a tour of Peter's Place, starting in the barn, where they met Roger. Next, they walked over to look at the older cabin that served as a classroom, then on to the new one that housed the boys. When they returned to the front yard, Graham left them to talk to each other and made his way over to the corral, where Ryan and Jonah were working with the mares.

"Would you guys come with me?" he asked. "I have some people I'd like you to meet."

Both boys appeared reluctant to leave the horses and join the adults, but they followed Graham to where the teachers stood with Sasha, and the introductions were made.

Jonah, who always had an opinion and a comment to

make, was both solemn and respectful when he shook hands with Coach Atwater.

"I hear you play baseball and that you have a pretty good arm," the coach said. "I'd like to see you pitch."

"I don't have a mitt. All my stuff is still at my mom's house." Jonah shrugged a single shoulder. "I didn't think I'd have much use for it on a horse ranch."

"Not to worry," Atwater said. "I have a bat, balls and a couple of mitts in the trunk of my car."

"I haven't done any pitching in a while," Jonah said, "so I'm probably a little rusty."

"No problem. We can play catch until you loosen up." Atwater placed a hand on the boy's shoulder. "Come on."

Graham watched the coach and the hopeful pitcher stride toward the silver Chevy Malibu. Hopefully, Jonah was as talented as he said he was. Either way, Graham suspected that just knowing he had a chance to play baseball again might keep him on the straight and narrow.

At the sound of Sasha's voice, he turned to see her talking to Mrs. Stewart. Her arm was draped around Ryan's thin shoulders.

"It's nice to meet you," the teacher said. "From what I hear, you're a math and science whiz."

"He'd also like to attend a four-year university after graduation," Sasha added.

Ryan didn't appear to be nearly as enthusiastic about the topic as the adults talking to him, but he seemed to listen respectfully.

"You know," Mrs. Stewart said, "it's never too early

to check into grants and scholarships. In fact, if you join our math and science club, you'll get a lot of information to help you in selecting which university you'd like to attend, as well as everything you need to know about financial aid."

Ryan used his index finger to adjust his glasses. "I might be interested in joining that club."

For the first time since arriving at the Galloping G, the boy stood tall, his shoulders not the least bit hunched.

Graham would like to have seen a whopping big smile on his face, but he'd settle for the fact that Ryan no longer looked so beaten down.

He glanced at the side of the barn, where Coach Atwater knelt, a catcher's mask on his face, a glove in his hand. Jonah took a pitcher's stance, then wound up and threw a fast ball.

Hey. That wasn't bad. Things appeared to be working out nicely today—thanks to Sasha, who'd made it all happen. She was a natural-born social worker and would do a fine job counseling the kids at Peter's Place.

If things continued to develop between her and Graham, he wondered how she'd feel about him leaving. Not that he was in a huge rush to go now, but he did have plans of his own and wanted to utilize the MBA he'd earned.

He wouldn't abandon her, Roger and the boys, though. So, for the time being, he was committed to remaining on-site.

Thump!

At the sound of a baseball striking dead center in

a catcher's mitt, Graham turned to watch Jonah's try-out. Atwater returned the ball, and Jonah wound up for another pitch, this one a curve that again landed dead center.

"Whoo!" Atwater said. "That was a nice one."

Graham was impressed, too. He folded his arms across his chest and burst into a grin. He hadn't expected things to go this well. When he glanced at Ryan, he spotted the hint of a smile, something he'd wondered if he'd ever see.

Sasha had scored a big success today. Both boys seemed to realize they now had an opportunity to create a better future than the one they had been facing when they arrived.

Of course, they weren't out of the woods yet. In spite of the strides the boys had made so far, there was still a lot of work to be done. Graham also knew that some of the boys who came to stay at Peter's Place wouldn't settle in and transition this easily. There were bound to be struggles and possibly complete failure.

Brad Taylor had, however, said he'd be sending the teenagers who'd be more likely to benefit from living and working in a rural ranch setting. Still, there were no guarantees.

Graham glanced at Sasha, at the way the sun glistened off the white-gold strands of her hair, at the way her eyes twinkled when she studied her first two troublemakers and watched as they seemed to come around.

If truth be told, he was beginning to see an unexpected future for himself, too. He just hoped Sasha would be a part of it.

Chapter Ten

Graham, who was leaning against the corral and watching Jonah brush Ginger's coat, was about to tell the boy it was time to finish and clean up for dinner when a sleek black Town Car drove into the yard and parked near the barn.

The driver, who wore a dark sports jacket and slacks, got out of the late-model luxury vehicle and opened the door for the passenger in the backseat. He reached out his hand to an elegant older woman dressed in an expensive, cream-colored pantsuit and helped her exit.

The pair had either made a wrong turn and was lost, or Kate Fortune had decided to pay Graham a visit.

Who else could it be?

He pushed away from the corral and went to meet her. From what he'd heard, she'd celebrated her ninetieth birthday at the beginning of the year, although he'd never know it by looking at her. If he had to guess, he'd think she was in her late sixties or early seventies. No doubt that was due to her daily use of the Fortune Youth Serum, which she'd developed. Now she was a living advertisement for the product that had made her a billionaire.

She reached out a bejeweled hand to shake his. "I'm Kate Fortune. You must be Graham Robinson."

"Yes, ma'am. It's nice to meet you."

She smiled, her crow's-feet deepening a wee bit. "I'd heard you were much more than a cowboy, but you certainly look the part."

He didn't see any point in responding. Or in arguing.

She wore only the hint of a smile as she gave him another once-over. "I've heard a lot of nice things about you."

He'd heard plenty about her, too. She was an astute businesswoman, successful and well respected.

"Do you know why I'm here?" she asked.

"I have a good idea. Word's out that you've been making the rounds, visiting all the Fortune relatives. Apparently, you're giving the Robinsons the same courtesy."

"Yes, but just so you know, I'm not convinced that your father is really Jerome Fortune."

"I can understand your skepticism. But I'm convinced. Either way, it really doesn't matter."

"Why do you say that?"

He gave a single shoulder shrug, much like the way Jonah might have done. "I have my own life, my own dreams. And they don't revolve around the Robinsons or the Fortunes."

She studied him a moment, then said, "You'll find that I'm fiercely devoted to my company and equally committed to my family."

"I don't doubt it." In fact, he admired that about her.

Kate glanced at the corral, where Jonah stroked the mare's neck. At the same time, he batted at a fly with his free hand. As he did, the waistband of his new pants slipped low on his hips. The kid was going to need a belt or to have his britches altered.

"Anyway," Kate said, dragging Graham's attention back to her visit. "I believe you're bright, honest and fair. You also seem to be less invested in being a Fortune than the others."

That was true, but he refused to address any of her assumptions. Instead he said, "Thank you for the courtesy of an interview, which I'm sure is just a formality." It had to be obvious to her that, dressed like a cowboy, he wasn't boardroom material.

"I hear that you're developing a home for troubled teenagers," she said. "And it intrigues me. Would you mind showing me around?"

"Not at all." Maybe she'd like to make a tax-deductible donation. "We can start with a tour of the barn. But if you want to see the property, I'll get the Gator and drive you around."

"I'd like to see *everything*. Just let me slip on a pair of walking shoes."

Then a full tour it was.

Once she'd changed from her high heels, Graham took her into the barn and showed her the two horses stabled in the stalls, explaining the horse rescue part of their program. He also told her his and Roger's reason for creating Peter's Place.

"Two of the boys have already moved in," he added.

"I take it the young man who was brushing the mare in the corral is one of them."

"Yes, that's Jonah."

A grin tickled her lips, which bore a perfect application of red lipstick. "Perhaps you should take him aside and suggest that he'd do a better job if he pulled up his jeans and didn't show off his underwear."

Graham chuckled. "Actually, that's one of the new pairs we purchased for him recently. You should have seen how low he wore his old pants and just how much of his boxers showed."

"I can only imagine."

Graham took Kate out to the side of the barn and helped her into the Gator. While he drove her around the property, she seemed genuinely interested and asked a lot of questions, the kind a new buyer or another rancher might ask.

Apparently—and not surprisingly—Kate had done her homework before coming out here.

"Tell me," she said, "why haven't you purchased your own spread?"

"I might do that someday, but right now Roger needs me." The boys needed him, too, although he didn't mention it.

"You're very close to Roger Gibault." It was a statement, an assessment, it seemed.

Graham wasn't sure how deeply she'd researched his background, but she probably knew plenty already. So he merely said, "Roger is a good man. And he's been a second father to me."

He expected her to jump on his implication that Gerald Robinson, aka Jerome Fortune, had been lacking in the daddy department. But if she did, he'd keep his mouth shut. His old man didn't need any more bad press.

"Have you ever wanted to be a father yourself?" Kate asked.

Graham's foot nearly slipped from the gas pedal. How much did she know? And better yet, how much about himself did he want to disclose?

In spite of his usual preference to keep things close to the vest, he said, "Actually, I'd love to be a dad someday. I also think it would be cool to have a legacy to pass down to my children."

"But you don't work for Robinson Tech." Again, it wasn't a question, just a statement. And an accurate one at that.

Was she naturally so astute? Or had she been talking to someone? Either way, it was a fact, so he supposed it really didn't matter.

"I plan to make my own mark on the world," he said.

"With Peter's Place?"

"That's just a part of it. Creating a home for troubled kids, where they can work with rescued horses, is my way of honoring a friend—and his father. But I do plan to start my own business one day."

"What kind of business?"

"I have a few ideas, but nothing set in stone yet."

"Do those ideas have anything to do with ranching?"

"Not really." But he would like to have his own

spread someday. Maddie would like growing up on a ranch and having her own horse.

They continued the tour in relative silence, and Graham's thoughts remained on Sasha and her daughters, on his dream to make them a part of his life. In fact, he hadn't realized just how much he'd hoped that would all come to be until he found himself saying, "There's a little girl who lives here. I've been teaching her how to rope and ride, and it's been a lot of fun."

Mentoring that little cowgirl had given him an immense feeling of pride, and he felt like her stepfather already.

Actually, talking to Kate and showing her the ranch had helped him sort through a lot of things, like his feelings for Sasha and wanting to create a family with her and her daughters. For that reason, he was going to have to lay it on the line and tell her how he felt about her.

Once he did, maybe he could start building that legacy he wanted to share and start planning for the future.

"You know," he said, another thought coming to him, "I was never close to my father, so I never understood why he was so insistent that I work at Robinson Tech and why he was so upset when I refused. But I think I understand now."

"Does that mean you're having second thoughts about joining the firm?" Kate asked.

"No, not about that. But I do have a new appreciation for what my father was offering me."

As he drove the Gator back to the house, he stole a glance at the elegant older woman seated across from him, her hands clasped in her lap, a two- or three-carat diamond glistening in the sunlight. Her brow was furrowed, and she appeared to be deep in thought.

Had the situation been reversed, he suspected she might have quizzed him about his thoughts. But he wasn't about to ask her.

When they reached the yard, he pulled alongside the Town Car so she wouldn't have very far to walk. He would have helped her from her seat in the Gator, but her driver beat him to it.

Before getting out, she reached across the seat and shook his hand. "Thank you for your time, Graham."

"It was my pleasure."

"I just might like to make Peter's Place one of my charities. I'll be in touch." Then she climbed into the backseat of her car. Moments later, the vehicle had turned around and was heading down the drive.

What an interesting woman. And what a surprising visit. He hoped she would choose to fund Peter's Place. There was so much Roger could do with the ranch and boys' home if he had another wealthy benefactor besides the Fortune Foundation.

He needed to tell Sasha about the possibility of a donation from Kate. And yes, while he was at it, he also needed to share his feelings for her and his dreams for the future, for *their* future.

He glanced at the corral, where Jonah had been working with the mares. Neither of the boys were within sight, so he figured he'd better check on them first.

That heart-to-heart with Sasha would have to wait. But not for long.

* * *

When Graham came out of the barn after checking on Ryan and Jonah, he spotted another unfamiliar car parked in the front yard. He'd no more than started for the house when Roger walked out onto the front porch, the screen door slamming behind him. He shook his head, clearly miffed about something, then plopped his hat on his head and proceeded down the steps and into the yard.

Before Graham had a chance to ask his old friend what was bothering him, Roger said, "You better do what I'm doing."

Graham furrowed his brow. "What's that?"

"Keeping my distance for a while." He turned and headed toward the barn.

Before the man could stomp off, Graham grabbed him by the arm and stopped him. "What are you talking about?"

Roger grimaced, then nodded toward the house. "Gabe Smith is inside."

The news nearly knocked the wind out of Graham, and he found it difficult to breathe, let alone wrap his mind around what that might mean. "What's he want?"

"Apparently, he and Sasha have something to work out," Roger grumbled, then swore under his breath. "I hope she's not falling for a line of bull. She'd be a fool if she did."

Graham was the fool. He'd waited too long to tell her how he was really feeling.

But would that have mattered?

"As luck would have it," Roger said, "Maddie invited

the guy to stay for dinner. And since I'll be damned if I'll risk ruining the relationship Sasha and I just patched up, I knew better than to object."

"I take it he agreed to stay."

"Yep." Roger let out a *hmph*. "And wouldn't you know? I made a pot roast, and plenty of it. Too bad he showed up and screwed up everything. I wish I'd fixed Hamburger Helper or some other inexpensive, effortless meal."

"Well, what's done is done," Graham said. Yet a cloak of apprehension settled over him.

"Dang it," Roger said. "I just hope he doesn't plan to spend the night."

At that thought, Graham's gut twisted into a knot. He tried to shake it off but didn't have any luck. He glanced at the car parked in front of the house, then at the front door. There could only be one reason for Gabe's visit. He'd come to his senses and wanted Sasha back.

Graham felt compelled to bust right in on the two of them and tell Gabe he was the one who was too late. Graham and Sasha hadn't just been tiptoeing around an attraction; they were actually feeling something strong and lasting. They had chemistry. And they also had a history.

But Sasha and Gabe had two children, which was pretty damn binding.

Just for the record, Sasha had once told him, *it was Gabe who left.*

That meant their split hadn't been her idea. And that she would have stayed married to him otherwise.

I'll be the first to admit that our life together was

far from perfect, but I made a commitment to stick it out for the long haul.

No, Sasha had meant to hold on. She'd made her vows before God and everyone in attendance at their wedding. That had to mean something to her, too. And on top of that, she was a mother and had her children to consider.

Hadn't Graham's own mother done the same thing, even when faced with his father's numerous affairs?

His thoughts drifted to the conversation he'd had with his sister Zoe after the last Robinson family meeting, after he'd mentioned that he'd seen his father kissing the au pair.

Graham had told Zoe that he'd tried to tell their mom about his father's cheating, but she hadn't taken the hint.

Zoe hadn't been surprised and had come up with a reason for it. *She had eight kids and probably wanted to hold her marriage together. It's what most mothers would do, I guess.*

Would they? Given the chance to save her marriage, would Sasha decide to take Gabe back and try to make a go of it?

Hell, she was also pregnant and no doubt feeling an urge to nest. Besides, she might not want to go through labor and delivery on her own.

Either way, Graham wasn't going to hang around and watch it all unfold. Talk about pain and misery...

The sudden urge to escape from Sasha, the ranch, the painful emotion threatening to choke the life out of him was nearly overwhelming, so he turned to leave, although he didn't have any actual destination in mind.

"Where are you going?" Roger asked.

"I've got things to do," Graham responded as he continued to walk toward the barn. He might be able to find something to keep him busy in there.

Still, none of those chores were the least bit pressing. But that didn't matter. Nothing good would come of him meeting Gabe Smith face-to-face.

Instead of enjoying a big helping of Roger's pot roast, Graham remained in his cabin during the dinner hour and warmed up a can of chili beans. He served himself a bowl, then opened a box of saltines and a bottle of beer and ate in front of the television.

He tried not to think about what was going on back at the big house, while everyone sat around Roger's kitchen table and enjoyed a family-style meal. But it was impossible not to. What made things worse was that Graham couldn't do a damn thing about anything that was happening.

It was easy to imagine, though. Gabe was telling Sasha that he'd missed her and Maddie, that he'd come to realize his mistake in letting them go. He was undoubtedly promising to be the kind of husband and father he should have been.

If he meant what he said, and if he was able to pull it off, Sasha, Maddie and the baby deserved Gabe's best.

Graham's thoughts drifted to his own father, a man who'd reached out to mend fences on several occasions. His dad had even offered him a position at Robinson Tech, which Graham had refused.

During the talk with Kate Fortune earlier today, he'd

had an epiphany about fatherhood. And while he'd been thinking about Maddie and her baby sister at the time, he'd reevaluated a few things in his own life.

Should he reconsider his dad's offer?

Moving to Austin would certainly get him away from Sasha and his memories of her.

In spite of his reluctance to forgive his father and to accept any personal responsibility for the lousy relationship they'd had in the past, he reached for his cell phone and placed a call.

His dad answered on the third ring, apparently after looking at the lit display and recognizing Graham's number. "Well, I'll be damned. It's the prodigal son."

Graham had half a notion to make some kind of snide retort, but he had to admit that his father's tone hadn't been snappish or surly. And he really couldn't blame him for calling him that, especially since he felt like one most of the time.

"Yeah, it's me. I thought I'd call and…say hello."

His old man didn't respond. But then, Graham didn't approach him often, especially to chat. Still, it was probably time to change that habit.

"I also wanted to suggest we end the cold war," Graham added. "For what it's worth, I admire what you've built in Robinson Tech."

Again, silence stretched across the line. Gerald Fortune Robinson had never been one to keep his thoughts or opinions to himself, so it seemed safe to assume he was a bit taken aback by Graham's admission.

But then again, there were a lot of things Graham *didn't* admire, like his dad's philandering. But that wasn't something he wanted to address today. He knew the kind of work it had taken his father to succeed—especially if he'd walked away from his Fortune ties and made a success on his own.

"Are you having second thoughts about working with me?" Gerald asked.

Was he? "Let's say that I may have been stubborn in refusing to talk it over with you."

"Well, for the record, the job offer still stands."

"Thanks, I appreciate that." But did Graham dare to take it? Was he that desperate to escape Sasha and everything that reminded him of her?

"I really like what I've been doing here at the Galloping G. Things seem to be working out well. So I'd have to figure out a way to work with Roger from a distance. I'll have to give it some thought."

"Good. I'm glad to hear it. And I'm glad that MBA I paid for might actually benefit me and the company."

Graham had only said he'd consider it. "We'll have to talk it over the next time I'm in town."

"When do you think that'll be?"

"Soon." Graham didn't want to give him a date, which would lock him in before he was actually ready for a conversation like that.

Besides, each time he thought about what was going on inside the ranch house, he realized that even a move to Austin wasn't going to be a sufficient balm for his battered heart.

Sasha had missed Graham at dinner, but she knew he sometimes ate at home. And with her soon-to-be-ex-husband's unexpected arrival, that was probably for the best.

She couldn't believe Maddie had actually suggested he spend the night with them, but fortunately, when she'd suggested he'd be more comfortable at a hotel in Austin, he'd opted to get a room before flying home tomorrow morning.

She and Gabe still had a lot to iron out when it came to coparenting, but if he was truly trying to be a better family man, she was willing to work with him. They'd worked out a reasonable holiday visitation schedule and had agreed on the last legal issue, assuming both attorneys concurred. But she still wanted to run her thoughts by someone she trusted to offer her sound advice. Since Uncle Roger would be biased, she decided to speak to Graham.

She could have walked to the cabin, but her back had started to bother her about the time Gabe arrived, and after standing at the sink and doing the dinner dishes, she really didn't feel up to the effort. So she called Graham instead.

The phone rang four times. She was just about to leave a message on his voice mail when he answered.

"Hey," she said. "Are you hungry? We have plenty of leftovers here."

"Thanks, but I already had dinner."

She paused a moment, thinking he might expound on his answer, but he didn't.

"I'd like to talk to you," she said.

"That's not necessary. I understand completely. It was probably the best decision for you to make."

Huh? She bit down on her bottom lip and furrowed her brow. What decision was he talking about?

"Don't worry, Sassy. I don't want to stand between a man and his family, so I'll bow out gracefully. Have a good evening." He hung up before she could get a word in edgewise.

What in the heck had just happened?

Chapter Eleven

Sasha continued to hold the telephone receiver long after Graham ended their call.

She was stunned and still trying to make sense of what he'd told her, as well as his haste to end the conversation before it had even gotten started. Apparently, he'd assumed that she and Gabe had patched things up. He hadn't even taken the time to ask or to let her explain.

Had he just jumped on an easy out and used it as an excuse to cut bait while he had the opportunity?

Sasha was still standing in the center of the living room, befuddled and rubbing an ache in the small of her back, when her daughter sidled up to her.

Maddie wore her pink jammies and held her stuffed bunny. But her expression was splashed with concern. "What's the matter, Mommy?"

Sasha cupped a hand on her little girl's head, felt the silky strands of her hair. "Nothing."

"Are you sure?"

No, she wasn't. Everything appeared to be falling apart. But she didn't want Maddie to worry about anything, so she forced a smile and stretched the truth to the limit. "Yes, I'm fine. Now go to bed. I'll come in there in a few minutes to read you a story."

As Maddie padded down the hall, Sasha's thoughts returned to Graham and the conversation they'd just had. Or rather, the words he'd said, since he hadn't let her respond.

She'd called to tell him that her divorce would be final within the next two weeks. Gabe had only flown to Texas to visit, as he'd told her he would. He'd wanted to iron out those visitation issues and the one last detail.

Hadn't she explained as much to Graham? She'd thought so. At least, she'd tried to, but he'd jumped to the wrong conclusion.

Had he been looking for a way out? Had he gotten scared and realized that he didn't want to take on the responsibility of a husband and father? Not that he'd actually said as much, but...

Unable to focus on anything other than Graham's distant tone and brief response, she picked up the phone and called him again. But this time, it only rang once and went right to voice mail.

He'd shut off his phone?

Maybe he was on the line with someone else. Or his battery had run down. He might have turned in for the night.

She supposed there could be any number of reasons she hadn't been able to get through to him, but she wasn't buying any of them. In fact, she was tempted to march across the yard and talk to him in person. But in reality, she wasn't up for a confrontation tonight. Not after the stress she'd had while working out a fair and feasible holiday visitation with Gabe, a schedule that would require her to fly to California with the girls in November and then again in December.

Besides, her back ached something awful, and she wasn't about to do anything to make it worse.

What she really needed was a warm, relaxing shower. But first, she went through Maddie's bedtime ritual, taking time to read *Sleeping Ugly* and *The Paper Bag Princess*, her own favorite stories. Then she kissed her daughter good-night.

When Maddie tucked her bunny under her arm and rolled to the side, Sasha headed to the bathroom and took a relaxing shower. She remained under the spray of warm water until her backache eased. By the time she'd slipped into her cotton nightgown, she felt much better.

She climbed into bed and closed her eyes. But she didn't fall asleep for the longest time. She continued to think about Graham and the way he'd shut her out. As a result, she tossed and turned so much during the night that she woke with another ache in her back. She'd nearly forgotten the discomfort of those last six weeks before Maddie's delivery.

As much as she loved baby Sydney, and as eager as she was to see her and hold her in her arms, she couldn't help thinking that her pregnancy might have contributed to Graham having second thoughts. She could actually understand that, but he should have been honest with her.

By breakfast, she'd worked herself into a real stew and was spitting mad at Graham for withdrawing so abruptly and not allowing her a chance to speak or to explain.

Apparently, he chose to walk away from emotional conflict. He'd certainly done that with his own family.

And now he was doing it with *hers*!

She'd had so much hope for him, for *them*. She'd planned to talk to him about it privately after breakfast, but he didn't even show up for a cup of coffee.

Well, if he thought he could avoid her and ignore those blood-stirring kisses they'd shared, he was mistaken. There was no way she would roll over and let him get away with it. So she went in search of him and found him in the barn.

He was giving Jonah and Ryan a list of chores to do that day, so she waited for him to finish. Once the boys headed out, she caught his gaze.

"What's up?" he asked.

"We need to talk."

He lifted his hat, then readjusted it on his head. Had she unbalanced him by asking him to address his thoughts and feelings honestly? If so, good.

"About what?" he asked.

Seriously? He didn't have a clue?

She crossed her arms, resting them on the shelf her expanding womb provided. "You've been running from things all your life. And if you don't start facing your fears and conflicts, you'll never reach your full potential. On top of that, you'll also fall short when it comes to advising and mentoring the boys."

His brow creased, yet he continued to hold back his words, as well as his thoughts.

So she pushed on. "Graham, you have a master's degree in business administration and aren't really using it. Sure, Peter's Place is a noble project. And you've done wonders with it. But what about *you*? What will make you happy in the long run?"

His eye twitched, which was the first indication that her words hadn't just dissipated in the air.

"Don't worry about me," he said. "I'll be fine."

He couldn't have dismissed her any more thoroughly than if he'd told her to get out of his life. So she turned and walked away.

She doubted he realized it, but when push came to shove, she had her daughters to think about and a new family to create. And if that meant Graham wouldn't be a part of it, so be it. She just wished that it wouldn't hurt so badly to move on without him.

Graham remained in the barn long after Sasha left, trying to make sense of what she'd said. And why she'd said it.

What did Robinson Tech have to do with anything? His biggest problem right this moment had to do with Gabe Smith, who'd apparently driven off sometime after nine o'clock last night and before breakfast this morning. No telling where he'd gone or when he planned to return.

Graham might have asked Sasha where the guy had gone and when he'd be back—if he'd had the chance. But he'd been completely stunned by the accusations she'd launched at him. He'd never run from anything in his life, other than the current heartbreak over Sasha and her ex. And he wasn't afraid of his feelings. He just didn't wear them on his sleeve.

Besides, he'd talked to his dad yesterday and said he'd consider the job offer. Not that he actually planned to take it. But he'd given it some thought.

Graham swore under his breath, then headed out of the barn to check on the boys, who'd taken the mares out to graze in the pasture for a while. He'd been giving them more and more responsibility each day, and they were handling it just fine.

Rather than walk to where Jonah, Ryan and the horses were, he took the Gator. When he got within twenty yards of them, he shut off the engine and watched for a while. As he did, he felt a surge of pride. They'd clearly listened to his instructions and were doing a good job of gentling the mares.

Peter's Place is a noble project, Sasha had said.

Damn right it was. Yet it wasn't the only thing he wanted to do with his life. Sure, he'd serve on the board of directors and offer financial support. He'd also visit often. But he wanted to have more than just a "project."

If things had been different between him and Sasha, he might have put up an argument when she'd accused him of running from his feelings and responsibilities. But why should he have to defend himself? He might have been a rebel once, but he was proud of the man he'd become. And he was proud of his dreams.

Couldn't she see that?

Apparently not. Thank goodness he'd decided to let her go before he got any more involved.

"Hey, boss!" Ryan called out.

Graham, who'd been gazing in the distance, looked at the boy.

"Isn't that Maddie?" Ryan pointed across the field, where the little blonde pixie in a cowboy hat was following the dirt road he'd just driven.

"Yeah, that's her," Graham said.

But what was she doing out here all by herself?

He turned the Gator around and went to meet her. When he pulled alongside her and parked, she slapped her hands on her hips and shot him child-size daggers from her eyes.

She was usually happy to see him. So what was that all about?

"What are you doing?" he asked.

"Looking for you." Her expression softened a bit, but she was clearly on a mission. And he doubted anyone else had sent her on it.

"What can I do for you?" he asked.

"You made my mommy sad, and that wasn't very nice."

Graham didn't think Maddie had pegged her mom's feelings accurately. Sasha was clearly angry, although he wasn't sure what kind of burr had gotten under her saddle.

But whatever it was, it had affected Maddie enough

to send her out to find him and give him a piece of her mind. Or so it seemed.

Graham patted the seat next to him. "Climb up here and tell me why she's sad. And why you think it's my fault."

"Because she misses you. And so do I."

Graham let out a weary sigh. What was he supposed to tell the child? That he'd hoped to maybe be her step-dad someday? That he'd been crushed when he realized that wasn't going to happen?

"Did I do something to make you mad?" Maddie asked as she climbed into the seat next to him. "Is it my fault you don't want to eat with us or be with us?"

"No, of course not. What makes you think that it could possibly be your fault?"

"Because my daddy used to be cranky whenever he came home. And now that he doesn't live with us, he's nicer to us."

Graham wasn't about to defend Gabe Smith, but he didn't want the poor kid to think that she was responsi-ble for the mess he'd fallen head over heels into. "None of this has anything to do with you, sweet pea. When you're a little older, you'll understand."

"I don't have to wait until then. I get it *now*." She hung her head. "You're going to leave us, just like Daddy did."

"But your father came back."

She shook her head, her pigtails swishing back and forth. "Not forever. Just for last night. He went away again because Mommy told him to go."

Sasha asked Gabe to leave?

Was that what she'd meant to talk over with him? Had he connected the wrong dots and made a false assumption?

He'd been so caught up in his disappointment and sorrow that he'd thought...

Damn. He'd been wrong. No wonder she'd accused him of running from his feelings.

"Does your mom know you're here?" Graham asked.

Maddie shook her head, sending those pigtails waving again. "When I saw you leaving, I was afraid if I went into the house and asked for permission first, I wouldn't be able to find you."

"You shouldn't have wandered off without telling anyone." Graham reached for his cell to call the house, only to get a busy signal. Maybe the phone was off the hook. He tried Sasha's number next, but it rolled over to voice mail.

"Your mom is probably looking all over for you," he said. "I'll drive you back to the house."

"Will you please talk to her?" Maddie asked. "Will you tell her you're sorry?"

"You bet I will." He had several apologies to make, one of which was for keeping his feelings to himself, something he was determined not to ever do again. Especially with her.

As Graham pulled the Gator into the yard, he spotted Sasha on the porch, one hand on her baby bump, the other over her heart. She wore a pair of shorts, a pink maternity top and an expression that was a hodgepodge of emotions like fear, concern, apprehension.

"I have her," Graham said as he climbed from the Gator. "She's fine."

"Thank God." Yet Sasha remained on the porch. She removed the hand she'd had on her chest and reached for the railing as if she needed it for support and to hold her upright.

Graham made his way toward the woman he loved, prepared to go down on bended knee if he had to. "Now that Maddie's home safe and sound, I need to talk to you."

"I'm afraid that'll have to wait," she said.

It was then that he realized Maddie hadn't been the only thing that had her worried and apprehensive. "What's the matter?"

"My water just broke."

Graham had known that apologizing for being a stupid jerk and sharing how he felt about Sasha wouldn't be easy, but he hadn't expected to do it at the hospital between her contractions.

When she told him she was in labor, he'd practically stumbled up the steps to get to her, to offer her a hand to hold and a shoulder to lean on. And while she had to have been worried about having a premature baby, she'd already called the doctor and had packed an overnight bag.

Roger had agreed to stay at the ranch and watch Maddie while Graham had helped Sasha into his pickup and rushed her to the ER.

He'd apologized several times, but for the most part,

she merely nodded and made funny breathing sounds, which he assumed was some sort of Lamaze technique.

Oh, God. This couldn't be happening.

But it was.

Fortunately, the doctor had already prepared the hospital staff for Sasha's arrival. So once they entered the automatic doors to the ER, she was immediately whisked away and taken to the obstetrical ward.

Graham hadn't been about to let her go through labor alone, so he'd followed along at a steady clip.

"Thank you for being with me," she'd said during a break in contractions.

He reached for her hand and gave it a gentle squeeze. "I wouldn't be anywhere else, Sassy."

She blessed him with an appreciative smile, but it didn't last long. As another contraction struck, Graham continued to hold her hand, although her grip on his fingers tightened like a vise.

Fortunately, several minutes later, the doctor, a woman in her late forties, came in.

"I'm scared, Dr. Singh," Sasha admitted. "It's too early for her to be born."

"Five weeks isn't all that early," the doctor said.

As she began to slip on a pair of gloves, Graham removed his hand and stood. "I'll step out of the room."

"You won't leave me, though," Sasha said. "Will you?"

"No. I'm in this for the duration." And he didn't just mean labor and delivery. "I'll be standing outside the door."

Graham stepped into the corridor, but he didn't have

to wait very long. The doctor came out soon afterward, so he took a moment to ask his own questions. "Is everything okay?"

"Yes, Sasha's doing fine. I'm going to order an epidural, which will make her a lot more comfortable."

"Good. That's a relief. I hate seeing her in pain."

The doctor smiled. "This probably won't take very long. I suspect we'll have a baby in a couple of hours."

Graham was glad to hear that, especially if little Sydney was going to be okay. He thanked the doctor and returned to Sasha's bedside, where he remained until the anesthesiologist arrived to give her the epidural. But this time, he didn't leave the room.

Within a minute or two, Sasha settled back into bed, her pain all but forgotten.

"Now we just have to wait," she said.

"Actually, we also have to talk. I'm not sure if you heard what I was telling you in the pickup, honey, but I'm sorry for reacting the way I did when Gabe arrived. I know I acted like a complete jerk, but I thought for sure that he'd realized what an amazing woman you are. I assumed that he'd come to the ranch to tell you he was willing to do anything to hold his family together."

A wry smile stretched across her face. "You obviously don't know Gabe very well. He was somewhat apologetic, but he really doesn't want to be a full-time husband and father."

"The guy's crazy. I'd give anything to have a wife like you."

She shot him a look of surprise. But then, why

wouldn't she? He'd kept that secret locked up inside for way too long.

"I love you, Sassy. More than I ever thought possible. I should have told you before, but I was afraid to. Do you think you could give me a chance to prove that I deserve you, Maddie and the new baby?"

She smiled, and her eyes brightened. "Believe it or not, the only man I've ever really loved is you."

"Me?"

"I've loved you for years, Graham. Back when you didn't even know I existed."

He was glad to hear that, but… "What about Gabe?"

"I thought I loved him when I married him, but he wasn't the man I thought he was." She glanced at the monitor, watched as another contraction seized her, this one not causing any pain or discomfort. Once it started to subside, she continued. "I wish I could say I was heartbroken over our split, but that couldn't be any further from the truth. And the fact that Maddie didn't appear to be all that upset by the breakup certainly helped me come to the conclusion that a divorce was for the best."

"You have no idea how relieved I am to know that. When he arrived, I thought it meant that he was having second thoughts."

"Only about visitation. He'd like the girls to spend both holidays with him and his parents. So that means I'll have to go, too. And while I'm not happy about it, I agreed."

"If it will make things easier for you, I'll go along, too."

"Seriously?" Her expression morphed from disbelief to delight. "You'd do that for me?"

"I'd do it for all of us. I want us to be a family, Sassy."

She reached for his hand and gave it a squeeze. "I want that, too."

An hour later, the nurse returned to examine Sasha. And this time, she said, "It's time. I'll call the doctor and prepare the room for delivery."

Things happened quickly at that point. Graham had intended to step out of the room as the time got close, but Sasha asked him to stay. And in truth, he'd hoped she would.

He'd held her hand while she pushed her—no, *their*—new daughter into the world, a tiny, squalling little girl, with a red face, blond hair and a voice that was loud and strong.

"Is she okay?" Sasha asked the doctor.

"She looks great to me. She may have to stay in the NICU for a while, but I don't anticipate any problems."

Graham whispered a prayer of thanksgiving, then blew out a wobbly sigh. Being a new dad was a little scary, but it also felt good.

Sasha was able to hold baby Sydney for a moment, but the nurse soon took her to the NICU.

When they were finally alone, Graham placed a kiss on Sasha's forehead. "I'm so proud of you. Do you have any idea how much I love you?"

She smiled. "No, but I can't wait for you to show me."

He laughed. "Well, I realize some things will have to wait until you're fully recovered. But just know that I plan to propose as soon as your divorce is final."

"There's nothing I'd like more."

Graham's heart filled to the brim. Things were certainly working out a lot better than he'd once thought.

"By the way," he said, "I'm going to spend the night with you tonight."

"Here? At the hospital?"

"If they'll let me."

"They will. I'm just surprised that you…" She bit down on her bottom lip, then slowly shook her head and grinned. "Well, darn, Graham. You've sure turned out to be a real trouper."

"Yeah, well, unlike Gabe, when I make a commitment, I stick by it. And that means I'm going to stay with you and the girls for the rest of my life."

Then he placed his lips on hers, sealing that vow with a kiss.

After Sasha called Roger and spoke to both him and Maddie, Graham decided he had a call of his own to make.

For some reason, becoming a father made him want to reach out to his own dad.

Gerald Robinson picked up on the third ring. "Well, I'll be. Two calls within a short period of time."

"Yeah, well, I wanted to let you in on my good news," Graham said. "I'm getting married. And you'll get not only a daughter-in-law but two instant grandchildren."

"Who is she?"

"Sasha-Marie Gibault, Roger's niece. I've known her for years, but we recently reconnected and fell in love."

"Well, if you're happy, then I'm happy for you," he

said. "But I have some news of my own. I've decided not to hide anymore. I met with Kate Fortune earlier today and told her the whole story about my past."

Graham would've loved to be a fly on the wall when that happened! His father had been hiding the truth for years, but at least he was finally admitting it.

"Kate had already suspected it," his dad admitted, "but she wanted to see how the story would play out."

"She's one sharp woman," Graham said.

"I agree. She also told me that she selected the person she wanted to run Fortune Cosmetics."

Graham assumed it would be one of the closer Fortune cousins, although now that his dad had come clean, he supposed he would add Fortune to the Robinson name, just as Ben and some of the others had done. Prior to that, he hadn't wanted to get caught up in the family drama.

"So, who did Kate choose?" Graham asked.

"You."

Graham nearly choked on the news. "That makes no sense. You must have heard wrong."

"I'm never wrong about anything," Gerald said, true to form. "Kate saw something in you and wants you to run her business. And for the record, I think she made a good choice."

His father's admission stunned him even further. He couldn't remember the last time his dad had acknowledged that he had any talent or admirable qualities. As much as he'd tried to convince himself over the years that it really didn't matter, that wasn't true.

"That's why I tried so hard to get you to come and work with me," Gerald added.

Now, that was a pleasant surprise. Graham had always suspected his father had only wanted to have some control over him.

"For the record," Gerald said, "I'm proud of you and what you've helped Roger do with the Galloping G. In fact, I'm going to make a sizable donation to the project."

"Thanks, I appreciate that." Graham glanced at Sasha, who'd dozed off. There'd be time to share his news with her later, although he wasn't sure he'd want to commute to Minnesota, where Fortune Cosmetics was located. Would she agree to move there with him?

"You might be happy to hear that Kate has enjoyed her time in Texas, away from the miserable winters. So she's going to move the corporate headquarters to Austin. She also said that her company is the kind that allows for job sharing and working from home. So that means you can remain close to Roger and the ranch."

Wow. Graham didn't know what to say. He didn't know anything about cosmetics, but he wasn't afraid to learn. Not when Kate was offering him the chance to work alongside her in a billion-dollar company and utilize his MBA. So there was no reason not to accept her offer.

"That's good news," he said to his dad. And he wasn't just talking about the job. The fact that Gerald had admitted his relationship to the Fortunes meant that Graham could do so, too. He'd also use his ties with the Fortunes and the Fortune Foundation to build

Peter's Place into the kind of ranch he and Roger had envisioned it to be.

"Listen," Gerald said, "I have a meeting I have to attend. But I'll stop by the ranch to meet your fiancée and my new grandchildren soon."

They said their goodbyes, then ended the call.

As Graham slid his phone back into his pocket, he turned to Sasha and watched her sleep.

How strange life could be. And how wonderful. Before long, he'd marry the woman he loved with all his heart.

The future had never looked brighter.

Chapter Twelve

Four months later, as fall settled over Austin, turning leaves to crimson and gold, Graham and Sasha turned into the long driveway that led to the Silver Spur. Kate Fortune and her husband, Sterling Foster, had recently purchased the exclusive ranch where Kate had celebrated her ninetieth birthday at the beginning of the year.

According to Graham's sisters, the house was amazing and the grounds pristine. Yet Kate and Sterling planned a big remodel, after which, they would rename it Sterling's Fortune.

Sasha glanced out the window and spotted several Thoroughbreds grazing in a lush, green pasture framed by a white fence. The Silver Spur certainly didn't resemble any of the ranches she'd ever visited. In fact, it was impressive by anyone's standards, and she could scarcely take it all in.

Neither could she believe that Kate was hosting a wedding reception for her and Graham here. They'd married quietly this afternoon, with only Uncle Roger and a few close friends and family members in attendance. But Kate had insisted they needed a "real" celebration, and from what Sasha had gathered, no one argued with Kate.

"We're here," Graham said as he pulled into the circular drive, where a valet service had been set up to handle the parking.

Maddie, who sat in the backseat next to baby Sydney, said, "Wow. Is this where the queen lives?"

She certainly does, Sasha was tempted to say, since Kate Fortune clearly lived like one. Instead she smiled at her daughter and said, "No, honey. But it does look like a palace, doesn't it?"

As the valet opened the door first for Sasha, then for Maddie, Graham unlatched the baby carrier from the bottom part of the car seat and carried it with him. They could have found a sitter, but Graham thought this should be a family affair. And Sasha agreed. Even Uncle Roger was coming today, although he'd insisted upon driving himself.

The new family climbed the steps, which were flanked by stone pillars, to the front door. Graham rang the bell, and a butler wearing a black suit and a polite smile answered and welcomed them into the marble-floored entry.

"Sterling," Kate's voice rang out as she swept down a

circular stairway. "Hurry up, dear. Our guests of honor are here."

She greeted them warmly, then turned to Maddie and smiled. "Look at you in that gorgeous dress. You look as pretty as a princess."

"Thank you." Maddie, who did indeed look the part in her pink vintage flower-girl dress and the party shoes she'd also worn to the wedding, gave a little curtsy. "And you look like a *queen*, Miss Kate."

They all laughed, but there was a lot of truth to her statement. Kate looked elegant, as well as lovely.

She'd also been incredibly kind to Graham, taking him under her wing and sharing her business acumen. She'd told him that Fortune Cosmetics needed someone of his caliber on board. And when he'd mentioned that Sasha planned to stay on at Peter's Place, she agreed with Graham that he needed to continue at the Galloping G for the indefinite future.

In the meantime, he would be her consultant at Fortune Cosmetics until he felt comfortable taking over as CEO.

"I know this party is to celebrate your marriage," Kate said, "but I plan to announce your new position in the company. I hope that's okay with you, Graham."

"Of course," he said. "And again, I want to thank you for the opportunity."

"You're welcome. Now come with me and see how we've decorated for the reception." She led them into a large room cleared of the typical furniture. Instead round banquet tables draped in white linen and topped with bouquets of red roses and fine china and crystal had been set up.

She hadn't spared any expense, or so it seemed. But from what Sasha had heard, she could well afford it.

The doorbell rang, and Kate said, "It looks like the guests have begun to arrive. Please excuse me while I greet them."

When she left the room, Sasha turned to Graham. "I can't believe she even offered us the use of her private jet and had planned to spring for a honeymoon."

"I told her we couldn't leave the kids," Graham said. "But don't worry, Sassy. We'll have plenty of opportunities to fly anywhere you want to go in the next few years."

"I know." She lifted her mouth to his, giving him a kiss before the guests, many of them Fortunes, began to trickle in.

And that was exactly how they began to arrive, in a steady stream. First came Graham's brother Ben and his lovely pregnant wife, Ella, along with Ben's twin, Wes, and his fiancée, Vivian. Both couples welcomed Sasha into the family, taking time to compliment Maddie and to coo at Sydney.

Sasha was glad to see Graham's siblings and their significant others becoming closer than ever before. Once Gerald had come clean and admitted who he really was, the meetings the Robinson siblings had begun to have earlier this year had gone from stressful to friendly, and she hoped they would continue to gather on a regular basis. Family was important, and she was glad she'd been so warmly accepted as a Robinson and a Fortune.

Chase Parker and his wife, Lucie, arrived next, followed by Lucie's brother, Charles Chesterfield Fortune, who held his son, Flynn, in one arm and clasped his fiancée Alice's hand with the other. Joaquin and Zoe Robinson Mendoza soon joined them.

The room stilled momentarily when Graham's parents entered the room. Gerald Fortune Robinson, also known as Jerome Fortune, was in his midseventies and still a dashing and handsome man. With salt-and-pepper hair, dark eyes and prominent eyebrows, he reminded Sasha of Sean Connery. He had his hand on Charlotte's back when they entered, but immediately removed it. He nodded at Graham and Sasha, but headed for one of several bars that had been set up along the perimeter.

Charlotte, also in her midseventies, had short, platinum blond hair and green eyes. While she bore a regal appearance and had a penchant for pearls and designer pantsuits befitting a Texas millionaire's wife, she seemed to be even more in vogue today. Yet she didn't immediately seek out Graham or Sasha. Neither did she join her husband at the bar. Instead she snatched a glass of red wine from a silver tray one of the waiters carried.

Before long, the house was abuzz with family, not only those who'd once thought they were just Robinsons, but also the ones who'd recently learned of their Fortune connection, like the Hayses, Chesterfields and Joneses. Then, of course, there were those who'd always known they were Fortunes.

Twenty minutes later, Kate rang a sterling silver bell, and everyone hushed.

"I have an announcement to make," she said. "I've chosen Graham Fortune Robinson to run my company."

Murmurs and a few "congratulations" followed. Apparently, she'd kept that news to herself. And Gerald, who'd been the one to tell Graham, had been sworn to secrecy.

"You might wonder how I made my decision," Kate said. "I realize Graham isn't a typical corporate man, but I observed the way he ran Peter's Place and the way he worked with the boys. I admire his even temper and his openness to new ideas. Most of all, I believe he has an appreciation of family that even goes above and beyond what I've seen in everyone else, which, of course, is more than admirable."

A spontaneous round of applause sounded, after which Graham spoke up. "I want to thank Kate publicly for the faith she has in me. I won't let her or Fortune Cosmetics down."

"I'm sure you won't," Kate said. "I also want to take this time to announce that another member of the family, Lucie Parker, will be overseeing a new branch of the Fortune Foundation, which will open in Austin within the next few months."

As Lucie smiled and nodded, Chase grinned proudly, slipped his arm around his wife and drew her close.

Kate cleared her throat, commanding everyone's attention once more. "I also want to apologize to Gerald on behalf of the entire Fortune family for the mistreatment he experienced when he was younger. Family may not always get along or see eye to eye, but I can't imagine how badly things must have been for him to turn his back on them entirely. And I promise that, going forward, the Fortunes will be there for Gerald and the generations of Fortune Robinsons to come."

That last announcement was greeted with applause by almost everyone in the room.

Was Sasha the only one who'd glanced at Graham's parents and caught the scowl on Charlotte's face? But then again, the woman had been through a lot during her thirty-five-year marriage, some of which couldn't have been pleasant. Sasha didn't think many women could adjust to changes like that easily.

"You know," Kate continued, "over the course of my life, I've seen and experienced quite a bit. Twenty years ago, I was kidnapped and left for dead. I never thought I'd live to be ninety or to see so many of my relatives find love, marry and start new generations of Fortunes." She smiled as she scanned the room. "My experiences since coming to Texas six months ago have far exceeded my expectations. There are so many family members here with diverse personalities and talents, I now feel even more confident that the Fortunes will prosper long after I'm gone.

"*Although*," she added with a wink, "thanks to Fortune's Youth Serum, that might not be for quite some time!"

As laughter erupted in the room, she nodded at several waiters, and they began to pass out flutes of champagne.

When everyone had a glass, including Maddie, who'd

been given sparkling apple cider, Kate asked them to lift their drinks in a toast.

"To the Fortunes!" Kate said. "I can't wait to see what you all do next."

Crystal clicked upon crystal, ringing out in celebration, as everyone chimed in, "To the Fortunes!"

"Now let the wedding reception begin," Kate said as she made her way to Graham and Sasha.

"I realize you didn't feel comfortable about leaving town while the baby was so young," she said. "But I've set up a honeymoon suite for you two here. I also took the liberty of talking to Graham's sisters, Zoe, Rachel, Sophie and Olivia. And they're more than happy to watch over the girls for the next day or so. I believe they had to draw straws for the opportunity, and Zoe won."

Graham turned to Sasha. "Kate mentioned the idea to me earlier, so I packed a bag for us, as well as one for the girls."

"Zoe has a fun and entertaining evening planned," Kate added. "She told me that she purchased *The Gingerbread Man*, which she plans to read to Maddie. Then they'll make and decorate gingerbread cookies. I believe there's also a Cinderella movie involved."

"So, what do you say?" Graham asked Sasha. "It's up to you."

"I'm stunned. First by Kate's wonderful offer, then by Zoe's enthusiasm." She reached out and embraced Kate. "Thank you for all the kindness you've shown us."

Then she turned to Graham, her husband, the love of her life. "I can't believe you were involved in the planning and that you were able to help pull off such an amazing surprise."

A smile stretched across his handsome face. "I take it that's a yes."

She rose on tiptoe and pressed a kiss on his lips. "It most certainly is! I'd love to have a honeymoon with you here."

And thanks to Kate Fortune, tonight would be a night to remember.

Several hours later, as the guests began to file out of the Silver Spur and head home, the newlyweds looked forward to their wedding night.

Sasha had felt a little uneasy about leaving the girls at first. But Maddie had been so excited about her first sleepover with Aunt Zoe and Uncle Joaquin. And baby Sydney was already on a good schedule and sleeping through the night. Besides, Zoe assured her they'd be just a short walk away in one of several guest quarters on the property.

So how could she possibly give it another worrisome thought? Once she'd agreed, her heart soared in anticipation.

When Graham asked where they were to go, Kate had pointed to the back door and beyond.

"You can't miss it," she said. And she'd been right.

The "honeymoon suite" had been set up in one of the smaller cottages. White twinkly lights adorned the trees in the front yard, while flickering votive candles lined the walkway. The forest-green railing that surrounded the small porch also sported festive little lights that blinked and winked at Sasha and Graham as they made the walk from the main house.

On the porch, two ceramic pots filled with bright red geraniums flanked the green door. Graham had no more than used the key to unlock it when he turned, swept Sasha off her feet and carried her inside.

"I declare, Mr. Fortune Robinson, you're even more gallant and chivalrous than I thought."

He laughed. "Just wait and see how romantic and loving I can be."

Once inside the small, cozy living room, where a fire blazed in the hearth and candles flickered on the mantel, he set Sasha's feet back on the hardwood floor.

She scanned the cozy room, amazed at what Kate had prepared for them. A bouquet of red roses sat atop the glass-topped coffee table, along with a sterling-silver ice bucket holding a bottle of Cristal champagne and two flutes. A tray of chocolate-dipped straw-berries, as well as an array of crackers and cheese, rounded out the display.

Kate had thought of everything, including an MP3 player. Something told Sasha that the kitchen would be stocked as well, with coffee, orange juice and a variety of sweet rolls and breakfast foods.

After Graham carried in their bag and placed it in the bedroom, he called out, "Honey, if you think the living area is nice, you ought to see this."

Sasha joined him, noting the king-size canopy bed that was draped with a white goose-down comforter that had been sprinkled with rose petals.

The backside of the fireplace they'd seen in the living room opened up in the bedroom, allowing both rooms to enjoy the roaring blaze. To round it out, there was a whirlpool tub, with a stack of white fluffy towels and two robes awaiting them.

"I can't believe this," she said. "It's awesome."

"And tonight, it's ours." Graham crossed the room to the MP3 player. Soon a love song filled the room with soft music, setting a romantic tone.

"I don't even know where to start," she said, thinking of the champagne and strawberries, along with the whirlpool and the bed.

"I know where to start." Graham swept her into his arms and kissed her, lightly at first, and then deeper, hungrier.

As she drew him close, as his tongue delved deeply into her mouth, mating with hers, she had to admit he'd made a perfect choice.

Their bodies pressed together, setting off a heady rush of heat through her blood. Their hands stroked each other, caressing and stimulating a ragged ache in her core.

The times she'd imagined how special their lovemaking would be, how amazing and heart-stirring, paled next to what they were sharing this evening. Their honeymoon would finally unite the two of them as one. And the bond would last not just tonight, but forever.

Graham led her to the bed, where he kissed her again, long and deep. His hands slid along the curve of her back and down the slope of her hips. Then he pulled her forward against his erection, letting her know how much he enjoyed claiming her as his wife, his lover and his lifetime partner.

* * *

When Graham thought he was going to die from the strength of his desire for Sasha, she ended the kiss, then slowly turned her back to him and lifted her hair out of the way so he could unzip the classic black dress she wore.

As he helped her peel the fabric from her shoulders, he kissed her neck, his tongue making small circles in the tender spot behind her ear.

She removed the dress completely and let it drop into a pool on the floor, then stepped out of it.

Beautiful Sasha was his, now and forever.

He unbuttoned his shirt and withdrew his arms from the sleeves. Then he tossed the garment aside. Next he unbuckled his belt and unzipped his slacks.

When he'd removed all but his boxer briefs, he eased toward her. She skimmed her nails across his chest, sending a shiver through his veins and a rush of heat through his blood.

But he wasn't the only one fully aroused and ready. She swayed at his touch and had to hold on to him to remain steady. But he took mercy on her, and on them both, lifted her into his arms and placed her on top of the bed.

Surrounded by rose petals, and with her hair splayed upon the pillow, she looked like a dream come true. *His* dream.

His wife. His Sasha.

Graham wanted nothing more than to slip out of his boxers and feel her skin against his, but he paused for a beat, drinking in the angelic sight. "You're the best thing that's ever happened to me, Sassy. And I love you more than you'll ever know." Then he bent over her and brushed another kiss on her lips.

She pulled him close. All he could think to do was to climb into bed with her, to trail kisses from her neck to her belly and lower.

Torn between driving her wild with need and needing to be inside her, he climbed next to her and continued to prove just how much he loved her. And how much they needed each other.

"I can't believe how special this is," she said. "Or how amazing this night will be."

"I plan to make every night special for you, starting now." Unwilling to prolong their foreplay any longer, he hovered over her.

She reached for his erection and guided him right where he belonged. He entered her slowly at first, relishing the slick, warm feel of her. As her body responded to his, as she arched up to meet each of his thrusts, their honeymoon began in earnest.

Time stood still, and nothing mattered but the two of them and what they were doing to and for each other.

As Sasha reached a peak, she cried out, arched her back and let go, taking him with her. Their climax exploded into a swirl of stars, bright lights and colors. He thrust one last time, shuddered and released along with her.

Making love had never been like this before, two hearts, two lives, two dreams, all melded into one.

As Graham held his new wife close, they celebrated their newfound fortune: each other.

Forever.

For always.

From this night forward.

* * * * *